LIFE AND ADVENTURES

OF

JACK ENGLE:

AN AUTO-BIOGRAPHY

A STORY OF NEW YORK AT THE PRESENT TIME IN WHICH THE READER WILL FIND SOME FAMILIAR CHARACTERS

WALT WHITMAN

with an introduction by

ZACHARY TURPIN

UNIVERSITY OF IOWA PRESS
IOWA CITY

University of Iowa Press, Iowa City 52242

uipress.uiowa.edu
Printed in the United States of America
Design by Sara T. Sauers

The University of Iowa Press is a member of Green Press Initiative and is committed to preserving natural resources.

Printed on acid-free paper
Library of Congress Cataloging-in-Publication Data is on file at the Library of Congress.

ISBN: 978-1-60938-512-5 (cl)
ISBN: 978-1-60938-510-1 (pbk)
ISBN: 978-1-60938-511-8 (ebk)

Cover image used with permission from Granger Historical Picture Archive, www.granger.com.

Frontispiece image courtesy the Thomas Biggs Harned Collection of the Papers of Walt Whitman, 1842–1937, Library of Congress, Washington, D.C.; digital image courtesy of Walt Whitman Archive (whitmanarchive.org).

ACKNOWLEDGMENTS

WITHOUT THE tireless efforts of Stefan Schöberlein, Stephanie Blalock, Ed Folsom, Karen Copp, Susan Hill Newton, Allison Means, Holly Carver, Sara Sauers, and Jim McCoy—all of the University of Iowa—this book would not be half so handsome as it is, nor anywhere as accurate. Furthermore, without the backing of the University of Houston English Department, in particular the unhesitating support of longtime chair Wyman Herendeen, *Jack Engle* might have lain indefinitely in the Library of Congress. The latter institution deserves special thanks as well, for its repository of Whitman manuscripts and ephemera and for the assistance of senior information and reference specialist Chamisa Redmond, a kind and unerringly helpful advocate in the archive. My gratitude also goes out to Erin C. Singer, Lesli Vollrath, Jason Berger, Michael Snediker, Karen Karbiener, Jerome Loving, Jason Stacy, and Doug Noverr, all of whom provided excited counsel and proved just how well they can keep a secret.

To my wonderful wife, Markie McBrayer, who helped me every step of the way, I owe no less than a puppy. Finally, this book is dedicated to our sons, John and Henry—a new generation of readers.

INTRODUCTION

by Zachary Turpin

WALT WHITMAN towers over poetry today, thanks to his masterwork, *Leaves of Grass*. Arguably no other American book has had a more profound influence on literature; with very few exceptions, every poet of the twentieth and twenty-first centuries owes something to Whitman, from Edgar Lee Masters to Anne Sexton, Hart Crane to Juan Felipe Herrera, Allen Ginsberg to Ai. As he would say, "I moisten the roots of all that has grown." At times, the entirety of modern poetry has been variously credited to (or blamed on) Whitman, the sheer improbability of which has had poets shaking their heads for generations. "One Whitman is miracle enough," gushed Randall Jarrell, "when he comes again it will be the end of the world." Even naysayers like Ezra Pound had to admit that the poet "broke the new wood." A workaday Brooklyn housebuilder-turned-bard, Whitman now rests in the American pantheon, a house he helped to build. His poetry permeates the American bookstore, the college curriculum, the culture itself, just as the name "Walt Whitman" permeates New England, plastered across high schools, bridges, avenues, tunnels, historic sites, walking tours, pubs, parks—indeed, a significant fraction of America bears his name, for as Pound said, "He *is* America." But because the Good Gray Poet's influence is so radical, it is easy to forget that he almost didn't become a poet in the first place.

At times, the young Whitman seems to have been unconvinced of his calling. At one point, he seriously considered becoming an orator, though he had no gift for it, and he knew it. At another, he enjoyed a decent living as woodworker, contractor, and job printer, even as *Leaves of Grass* gestated in his mind; he might have built houses indefinitely, had the market and his work ethic ever properly aligned. It was a good living. Yet his brother George later recalled of this time that Walt wanted more than a mere livelihood: "He never would make concessions for money—always was so. He always had his own way, or took it. There was a great boom in Brooklyn in the early fifties, and he had his chance then, but you know he made nothing of that chance. Some of us reckoned that he had by this neglect wasted his best opportunity, for no other equally good chance ever after appeared." Of course, with the benefit of hindsight, we may all thank our lucky stars that Whitman missed his "best opportunity" to be a housebuilder. At the time, though, it must have been a major blow to him. Whitman was short on cash and, undoubtedly, torn between the building he did by day and the writing he did by night. Would his little "leaves" ever amount to anything? Would he? What was likeliest to keep him and his family going? (Like many contractors of his day, Whitman and his family lived in the houses they made; they rarely called anyplace home for more than a few months.) Later in his life, these years of self-uncertainty were largely and perhaps conveniently forgotten.

As many Americans do in their thirties, Whitman agonized over his true calling. Because he had been in the newspaper business since the age of twelve, writing probably seemed the likeliest way to get steady work; by the early 1850s, he'd been employed by more than twenty newspapers, founding several himself. But while he loved the papers and thought of himself as a newspaperman, there is little indication that Whitman saw himself being a journalist forever. His editorial duties wore on him. "The stamp of the daily newspaper," he wrote privately, was hardly worth a cent, something "to be dismissed as soon as the next day's paper appears." It evaporated, leaving nothing to the ages. Whitman had a mind to create something more lasting, something more original, but what? A poem? A play? An opera? It may surprise readers to know that as he began writing what would end up as *Leaves of Grass*, Whitman seems to have had little or no idea in what genre he was writing or much concept of what his jottings would become.

Leaves of Grass was what America was—an impulse evolving into a shape, an experiment. In notebooks crammed with snippets and false starts, he ponders what form might capture the surge within: "Novel?—Work of some sort[,] Play?—instead of sporadic characters—introduce them in large masses, on a far grander scale—armies—[...] / nobody appears upon the stage singly—but all in huge aggregates / nobody speaks alone—whatever is said, is said by an immense number." The Whitman who would one day sing of himself, "I am large, I contain multitudes," sought a genre of writing equally multitudinous, and the choice was hardly clear. That *Leaves of Grass* might have ended up as a novel or a drama is a fact little considered today.

We probably have Whitman himself to thank for that—he was nothing if not a self-revisionist. As the genre of his opus gradually resolved itself into poetry, Whitman began to put a long and successful career as a writer of journalism and magazine fiction behind him. On July 4, 1855, he was reborn a professional poet, full-fledged: on that day there appeared in a handful of shops and reviewers' in-boxes a thin green book, the gilt letters on its cover spelling "Leaves of Grass." No author's name appears on the title page. Instead, there is only an etched portrait—a man looking out at the reader, beard graying prematurely, shirt unbuttoned at the top, hat tipped to the side, one hand in his pants pocket. This was no lordly Byron or wistful Keats. The rough staring off the page might as well be a deckhand or a bus driver or, what he was, a woodworker. And what sort of book is this, exactly? It does not immediately declare itself to be poetry. No subtitle announces "Poems" or "A Collection of Verses," so readers may take it however they like. The readers who noticed it in 1855 did just that and, generally, were either appalled or elated. Many would call it smut, street trash, unpoetic pornography. Rufus Griswold, a poet and editor already famous for slandering a freshly deceased Edgar Allan Poe, said of *Leaves* that "it is impossible to imagine how any man's fancy could have conceived such a mass of stupid filth, unless he were possessed of the soul of a sentimental donkey that had died of disappointed love."

Others saw in the book something entirely new. Ralph Waldo Emerson, Whitman's idol at the time, wrote the poet a glowing letter saying of the book that "I find it the most extraordinary piece of wit and wisdom that America has yet contributed." Emerson, then America's leading thinker and most famous man of letters, added: "I greet you at the beginning of a great career." (Whitman would print that last bit, without permission, on the spine of the book's second edition.) Here was a book, and here a poet, that might very well change the world. Whitman would spend the rest of his life, another three and a half decades, trying to do so, taking years to augment his book, revise and rearrange it, and promote it (and himself) as the herald of a new world, multicultural, democratic, all-embracing.

What the book does not embrace, however, is its literary heritage. Whitman constructed his *Leaves* to feel everywhere unprecedented, as new and experimental as the United States itself. This is why, stylistically, his poems often strike new readers as something they have never quite read before, though with the nagging sense of there being some echo of Shakespeare or Dante, Homer or the Bible. Influenced by all of these, nevertheless Whitman was merciless in revising away any overt reference or allusion to them, until what was left seemed derivative of nothing more than the sensations of nature, as told in a King James English salted with street slang. The influence of other genres, too, Whitman downplayed. He was a voracious reader of fiction, for example, having read "cartloads" of novels in his youth. "Indeed," he noted, "that was a most important formative element in my education." Yet he never once identified himself as a fiction writer, even though he wrote and sold nearly thirty popular stories before *Leaves of Grass*. It was during his tale-writing years (1841–1848) that he cut his writerly teeth, first with a temperance novel, *Franklin Evans* (1842), and later with a regular succession of stories and novellas from which he made a decent living. That the author of *Leaves of Grass* might have ended up a professional novelist is something Whitman seems to have taken care to underemphasize. This is why he almost certainly never told a soul that in 1852, at the age of thirty-three, he anonymously published a short serial novel, titled *Life and Adventures of Jack Engle*.

Many mysteries surround Whitman's life and work. Whether he suppressed some of his pulpier publications is not one of them. In the early twentieth century, finding lost writings by Whitman in whatever form—ghostwritten, published unsigned, handwritten in manuscripts or margins—was practically a cottage industry. Enterprising scholar-collectors recovered reams of anonymous journalism and bales of manuscripts, plus early poems, short stories, letters, and not a few reviews of *Leaves* ghosted by the poet himself. But there was little surprise in this. In life, even his most faithful apostles and executors suspected Whitman of holding out on them. He clearly knew the value of mystique; Whitman often promised his late-life friend and scribe Horace Traubel that he would one day reveal to him a "Great Secret." Whatever it was, Traubel never worked it out of him, though not for lack of prying. (Many scholars, myself included, believe the secret was the poet's sexuality.) But something else Traubel never learned was that the poet who wished his early fictions had "quietly dropp'd in oblivion" had, in fact, succeeded in submerging some of them himself—writings of which, since the moment of their publication, no one has been aware. This book is one of them.

Until 2016, *Jack Engle* was not merely missing but utterly forgotten—serialized, anonymously, in the pages of the *Sunday Dispatch*, one of countless New York newspapers that flourished and faded in the mid-1800s. Virtually no one has laid eyes on this story in a century and a half, certainly no one who knew what it was. Nor is *Jack Engle* the first Whitmanian secret to come to light. In 2015, readers were reintroduced to "Manly Health and Training," the poet's enthusiastically unrigorous health-and-wellness guide, which had been serialized and shut away in the *New York Atlas*. As far as anyone is aware, Whitman never spoke of it after its publication, and *Jack Engle* appears to have been published in similar secrecy. Indeed, if the poet's manuscripts tell us anything, even more books may be out there, waiting in the oblivion where he left them.

Plenty of American authors have left books in the dark. Writers from Ben Franklin to Stephen King have concealed themselves behind a good old-fashioned pen name. Often these hid nothing whatsoever, but occasionally they did. In the 1860s, A. M. Barnard published a dozen or so sexy, blood-soaked, gender-bending novels, potboilers with titles like *Behind a Mask*, *The Abbot's Ghost*, and *A Long Fatal Love Chase*. This would be otherwise unremarkable if two scholars, Madeleine Stern and Leona Rostenberg, hadn't discovered that "Barnard" was none other than Louisa May Alcott, the creator of such beloved works as *Little Women* (1868) and *Little Men* (1871). Alcott, a sometime seamstress and Civil War nurse, had been flush with more imagination than cash, it seems. The same can probably be said of Whitman in 1852, the year of *Jack Engle*. Though the Brooklyn housing market was at high tide, Whitman was having trouble staying afloat, a situation that would last until the end of the decade. The idea of a new profession, of being someone else, tied to something greater than the vicissitudes of middle-class homebuyers, is probably one of the inspirations behind the story of *Jack Engle*.

This is a novel about a man whose professional and personal destinies are incompatible, a tale of irony and coincidence. Readers familiar with *David Copperfield* or *Bleak House* will no doubt recognize many traces of Dickens. Our narrator-protagonist, Jack, is a plucky orphan whose early life he recounts as one of hardship and violence, occasionally illuminated by moments of genuine kindness from others. Those kindest to him are people who, like him, have little: shopkeepers, clerks, office boys, and orphans. In true Dickensian fashion, Jack's adoption is a key moment of innocence, and it is from this state of simplicity that he must mature into the complicated world of manhood. Jack's eventual entry into the study of law provides the necessary conflict: his employer, an unsavory lawyer named Covert, is gradually revealed to be a villain, who schemes after the inheritance of his adopted daughter, Martha. With the help of a band of merry friends, Jack sets out to save Martha, whose past he finds intriguingly bound up with his own. I will leave the rest of the book to the reader.

The tale of Jack's rise to maturity falls into the now-classic genre of the rags-to-riches story—or "rags to respectability," to borrow a phrase from scholars of Horatio Alger, Jr., the patron saint of such stories. Like Alger's dozens and dozens of novels about impoverished ragamuffins, *Jack Engle* tells the story of an orphan whose "luck and pluck" lift him out of poverty. However, what grants him respectability isn't his virtue or his work ethic but his sincere empathy with the poor and downtrodden. For that, this novel can be classified as a social reform novel, rather than an example of the now-well-established American myth of pulling oneself up by one's bootstraps. In this novel, no one is self-made. Indeed, Jack admits to being lazy, unsuited for nearly any sort of nine-to-five work, honest or otherwise—an autobiographical detail, to be sure.

Though it may go without saying, *Jack Engle* is not an "Auto-Biography," as its subtitle may claim, or anyway not a very strict one. Its broad strokes are certainly untrue. Whitman was never orphaned or adopted. He did not study law, though he did briefly clerk for a lawyer and his son. (Young Walter was twelve at the time.) It is also doubtful that Whitman ever had romantic relationships with women, despite his occasional undetailed assertions to the contrary. *Jack Engle* is, not to put too fine a point on it, fiction. Even so, it must be admitted that the story incorporates a few recognizable elements of the life of its author—including those that are key to understanding who Whitman was.

Geography strongly defined him. He was first and last a New Yorker, just as Jack Engle is—born on Long Island, raised there and in Brooklyn, and by the 1850s a regular visitor to Manhattan via the Brooklyn ferry, which he would later immortalize in verse. Other than a few trips across the western United States and to Canada, Whitman spent most of his life in New York City and Camden, New Jersey, just across the Delaware River from Philadelphia, the hub of American Quakerism. Since his early childhood, Quakers had meant a great deal to Whitman. He was not one himself, but his maternal grandmother was, so he considered himself "of Quaker stock." From childhood, he maintained a lasting interest in the Society of Friends, in their happy egalitarianism and lack of dogma; he attended a few Quaker meetings and at least once heard a speech by the great Quaker orator Elias Hicks. That *Jack Engle*'s central antagonist, Mr. Covert, is himself a Quaker is no doubt meant to be ironic. Like Ahab, Herman Melville's bloodthirsty pacifist, Covert is a contradiction—a chaste swindler, hardworking, respected, yet thoroughly underhanded. He is, in short, the stereotypical evil lawyer.

For personal reasons, Whitman seems to have despised lawyers. *Jack Engle* may now offer some clue as to why. In a little notebook (now housed at the Library of Congress) in which Whitman plotted out the novel's story, he reminds himself to include "some remarks about the villainy of lawyers—tell the story of Covert's father's swindling, about the house in Johnson st—damn him." Whitman once listed all of the childhood addresses he could recall, and beside "Johnson st. May 1st 1825"—where he had celebrated his fifth birthday—he noted: "Covert the villain." Chapter 7 of *Jack Engle* may help explain who this person was, and what he did to the Whitman family. In it, Jack's mentor and fellow clerk, Wigglesworth, reveals the unscrupulous ways of Covert. Long ago, the lawyer and his father had contracted with a "poor carpenter" to build a house, while casually waving away any suggestion that it be built on schedule. "Our carpenter was unsuspicious," the narrator explains, "and he took the matter very easily, until the arrival of the period mentioned in the contract." The contractual deadline passed, the Coverts refused payment, and inevitably "the lumber and hardware merchants levied for their bills, on the carpenter's own little property." The unnamed carpenter, head of a sizable family, lost everything, house and savings. Something similar seems to have happened to Whitman's father, Walter Sr., also a carpenter—and for this reason *Jack Engle* is clearly part revenge fantasy.

Truly, it is part everything. As with many of Whitman's major works, its genre is nearly impossible to identify. *Jack Engle* is a sentimental romance in one scene, a sensationalized adventure novel in the next. Whitman incorporates elements of autobiography, character study, suspense fiction, place painting, revenge narrative, morality tale, and detective fiction. At times his pace is slow, even meditative; notable in this regard is chapter 19, an abruptly thoughtful interlude among the gravestones of Manhattan's Trinity Church. But with little warning, Whitman easily shifts into the quick-paced, almost hammy style of a dime novel or yellowback: densely clichéd, heavily reliant on stereotype, with the occasional racist or sexist shorthand taking the place of finer-grained character development.

Nevertheless, this novel is something of a marvel. It is a marvel that Whitman ever wrote it; then as now, full-time contractors rarely found the time to write long-form fiction. It is even more a marvel that we have it. The *Sunday Dispatch,* in which *Jack Engle* appeared, is an exceedingly rare newspaper. It is neither digitized nor microfilmed, and very few libraries house more than one or two scattered issues. Of the six successive issues of the *Dispatch* in which *Jack Engle* appeared, only a single copy exists on earth today, in the Library of Congress. Were it not for that dedicated institution and the efforts of generations of literary executors, manuscript collectors, archivists, and scholars, this book might have been lost forever. But as Whitman reassures us, "Nothing is ever lost, or can be lost."

It is a philosophy I am beginning to believe. There is an infectious optimism in Whitman, something playful, encouraging, and good-natured. I suspect he would laugh at all of this. It may be shameful to admit it—at least as someone who now makes his living writing about the man—but until my late twenties I had hardly read a word of Whitman, poetry or fiction. Now I read him incessantly. As Whitman says, "I should have made my way straight to you long ago, / I should have blabbed nothing but you, I should have chanted nothing but you." There is something to be said for making up for lost time. Sometimes I find myself up late, while my family is asleep, looking for more Whitman. The Walt Whitman Archive is an online playground, filled with draft writings and page images and manuscript catalogs. It is impossible not to linger over the odds and ends, the scraps with no obvious connection to anything. There are hundreds of them. And after one spends weeks or months comparing dates, joining keywords, following trails, and sifting through old papers, eventually something may stand out as peculiar.

The peculiarity that led to this book was an advertisement. It appeared in the *New York Daily Times*—then a brand-new paper—on March 13, 1852. It looks like any other such ad, unsigned, poorly printed, hardly bigger than a modern business card. There is a name in it—"Jack Engle"—that seems to connect it to an old notebook of Whitman's, one filled with plot ideas and character names. But it is the ad copy itself that is remarkable. Promising "a rich revelation," it explains that

> This week's SUNDAY DISPATCH will contain the LIFE AND ADVENTURES OF JACK ENGLE, an Auto-Biography, in which will be handled the Philosophy, Philanthropy, Pauperism, Law, Crime, Love, Matrimony, Morals, &c., which are characteristic of this great City at the present time, including the Manners and Morals of Boarding Houses, some Scenes from Church History, Operations in Wall-st., with graphic Sketches of Men and Women, as they appear to the public, and as they appear in other scenes not public. Read it and you will find some familiar cases and characters, with explanations necessary to properly understand what it is all about.

It is after midnight. Asleep in bed next to me are my wife and newborn baby. I hold my breath. It may look unremarkable, but this ad is really something. The *Sunday*

Dispatch was one of Whitman's go-to newspapers. The year 1852 isn't out of the question. The character name is compelling. But there is something more about this little ad, something harder to put my finger on. Its overblown copy and absurdly comprehensive list of contents, its references to New York City, even the promise that the story has to be experienced to be understood—all this just *sounds* like Whitman. I've read plenty of Whitman's news copy, and I know, or think I do, what he sounds like when he is selling something. Or do I? Am I just projecting? In "Song of Myself," Whitman ends by looking back and beckoning. "I stop somewhere," he says, "waiting for you." Is Whitman somewhere beyond this newsprint, waiting? Art experts often swear they know when a painting is not a forgery but real, though they can point to no exact reason for this. Still, look at something long enough, read and reread it for any new sign, and any gut feeling starts to seem more like wishful thinking. What is real?

As it turns out, *Jack Engle* is the real thing, though that is still sometimes hard for me to believe. After an anxious month spent in correspondence with the Library of Congress, at last, graciously, I was sent an image taken of the *Sunday Dispatch*, and in a matter of seconds I could see that *Jack Engle*—this "auto-biography," this fiction, this mystery—matches perfectly the plot and characters in Whitman's old notebook. There is some truth in advertising, after all. *Jack Engle*, a new Whitman novel, written long after the poet is thought to have given up fiction, is every bit a "rich revelation." With it, a missing chapter in the poet's career as a novelist finally comes back to light. Indeed, there may be additional chapters left to find.

More than once, Whitman wrote himself notes preparing for some unknown piece of fiction. There is his warning, for example, to stick to "*a few Characters*, rather than many," and to construct "*the plot with one or two strong leading lines of interest.*" What is he referring to? As of now, no one knows. Whatever it is, Whitman reminds himself that it must be "*not too complicated*," with an emphasis on "dialogue—animation—something stirring." To me, he sounds for all the world like a storyteller setting out on another effort, an author planning to learn from his experiences. Could he have written yet another novel? I leave you with what Whitman said in old age, perhaps jokingly, perhaps seriously, about the trajectory of writers like himself: "In our time every fellow must write poems."

"And," he added, "a novel or two."

LIFE AND ADVENTURES OF JACK ENGLE

PREFATORY.—Candidly reader we are going to tell you a true story. The narrative is written in the first person; because it was originally jotted down by the principal actor in it, for the entertainment of a valued friend. From that narrative, although the present is somewhat elaborated, with an unimportant leaving out here, and putting in there, there has been no departure in substance. The main incidents were of actual occurrence in this good city of New York; and there will be a sprinkling of our readers by no means small, who will wonder how the deuce such facts, (as they happen to know them) ever got into print.

We shall, in the narrative, give the performers in this real drama, unreal names; and for good reasons, throw just enough of our own toggery about them to prevent their being identified by strangers.

Some of the faces embodied in the story have come to our knowledge from sources other than that above mentioned. These, we shall add, or withhold, as the interest of the detail may demand.

CHAPTER I.

An approved specimen of young America—the Lawyer in his office—Old age, down at the heel—entrance of Telemachus and Ulysses—a bargain closed.

PUNCTUALLY AT half past 12, the noon-day sun shining flat on the pavement of Wall street, a youth with the pious name of Nathaniel, clapt upon his closely cropt head, a straw hat, for which he had that very morning given the sum of twenty-five cents, and announced his intention of going to his dinner.

"COVERT
Attorney at Law"

stared into the room (it was a down-town law-office) from the door which was opened wide and fastened back, for coolness; and the real Covert, at that moment, looked up from his cloth-covered table, in an inner apartment, whose carpet, book-cases, musty smell, big chair, with leather cushions, and the panels of only one window out of three being opened, and they but partially so, announced it as the sanctum of the sovereign master there. That gentleman's garb marked him as one of the sect of Friends, or Quakers. He was a tallish man, considerably round-shouldered, with a pale, square, closely shaven face; and one who possessed any expertness as a physiognomist, could not mistake a certain sanctimonious satanic look out of the eyes. From some suspicion that he didn't appear well in that part of his countenance, Mr. Covert had a practice of casting down his visual organs. On this occasion, however, they lighted on his errand-boy.

"Yes, go to thy dinner; both can go," said he, "for I want to be alone."

And Wigglesworth, the clerk, a tobacco-scented old man—he smoked and chewed incessantly—left his high stool, in the corner where he had been slowly copying some document.

Old Wigglesworth! I must drop a word of praise and regret upon you here; for the Lord gave you a good soul, ridiculous old codger that you were.

I know few more melancholy sights than these old men present, whom you see here and there about New York; apparently without chick or child, very poor, their lips caved in upon toothless gums, dressed in seedy and greasy clothes, and ending their lives on that just debatable ground between honorable starvation and the poor house.

Old Wigglesworth had been well off once. The key to his losses, and his old age of penury, was nothing more nor less than intemperance. He did not get drunk, out and out, but he was never perfectly sober. Covert now employed him at a salary of four dollars a week.

Nathaniel, before-mentioned, was a small boy with a boundless ambition; the uttermost end and aim of which was that he might one day drive a fast horse of his own on Third avenue. In the meantime, he smoked cheap cigars, cultivated with tenderness upon his temples, his bright brown hair, in that form denominated "soap-lock," and swept out the office and ran the errands; occasionally stopping to settle a dispute by tongue or fist. For Nathaniel was brave, and had a constitutional tendency to thrust his own opinions upon other people by force if necessary.

Freed from the presence of the two, Mr. Covert sat meditating and writing alternately; until he had finished a letter, on which he evidently bestowed considerable pains.—He then folded, enveloped, sealed it, and locked it in his desk.

A tap at the door.

"Come in."

Two persons enter. One is a hearty middle-aged man, of what is called the working classes. The other is your humble servant, who takes all these pains in narrating his adventures, for your entertainment; his name is Jack Engle, and at the time of this introduction he is of the roystering age of twenty—stands about five feet ten, in his stocking feet—carries a pair of brown eyes and red cheeks to match, and looks mighty sharp at the girls as they go home through Nassau street from their work downtown.

"Mr. Covert, I suppose," said my companion.

"That is my name, sir. Will thee be seated?"

"My name's Foster," settling himself in a chair, and putting his hat on the table, "you got a line from me the other day, I suppose?"

"Ah, yes—yes," slowly answers the lawyer. Then looking at me, "and this is the young man, then?"

"This is the young man, sir; and we have come to see whether we can settle the thing. You see I want him to be a lawyer, which is a trade he does not much like, and would not himself have chosen. But I rather set my heart upon it; and he is a boy that gives in to me, and has agreed to study at the business for one year faithfully. And then I have agreed to let him have his own way."

"He is not thy son, I think I understood," said Covert.

"Not exactly," answered the other, "and yet so near the same as to make no difference. Now you know my mind, and as I am a man of few words, I should like to know yours."

"Well, we will try him, Mr. Foster, at any rate."

Then turning to me, "If thee will come in here to-morrow forenoon, young man, between nine and ten, I shall have more leisure for a talk; and we will then make a beginning. Although I warn thee in advance that it will depend entirely upon thyself how thee gets along. My own part will be nothing more than to point out the best road."

Which endeth the first chapter.

CHAPTER II.

The worthy milkman, and how he trusted people; and the wonderful luck he had one morning in finding a precious treasure.

THIS CHAPTER is necessarily retrospective of the preceding one.

Among the earliest customers of Ephraim Foster, there came one morning a little white-headed boy, neither handsome nor ugly. Ephraim kept a shop in one of the thoroughfares that cross Grand street, east of the Bowery; he sold milk, eggs, and sundry etceteras—in winter adding to his vocations, those of a purveyor of pork and sausage meat, which is a driving and a thriving trade, hereabout, in cold weather.

Fair America rivals ancient Greece in its love of pork. At the proper season, you may see, thickly set through the streets, the places for furnishing this favorite winter eating; beautiful red and white slices, mighty hams, either fresh or smoked, sides and fore-quarters—and, at intervals, a grinning head with fat cheeks and ears erect.—Still more preferable to some, is the powerfully spiced sausage meat, or the jelly-like head-cheese.

In the preparation of the latter articles, the worthy Ephraim always did wonders; for folks had confidence in him—which is a great deal to bestow on a sausage vendor.—However, he deserved it all. He deserved more. He was one of the best fellows that ever lived. People said now and then that he would never set the North River a-fire; and yet Foster jogged along, even in his pecuniary affairs, faster and steadier than some who had the reputation of much superior cunning. He was, without thinking of it at all, constitutionally kind, liberal, and unselfish. It was in an humble way, to be sure; but none the less credit for that.—He had a knack of making mistakes against his own interest—giving the customer the odd pennies, and never gouging in weight or measure.

Then although the usual sign of "No Trust" hung up over the counter, Ephraim *did* trust very much—particularly if the family asking indulgence were poor, or the father or mother was sick. Although this resulted several times in bad debts that were no trifle to a man in his sort of business, it was marvellous how in the long run he didn't really lose.

One time, a year after a certain thumping bill had been utterly despaired of, and the poor journeyman cabinet maker owing it had moved to another part of the city, things grew brighter with him, and he came round one cool evening to pay up like a man and make Ephraim's wife a pretty present of a work-box. Another time when the long,

long score of a poor woman, with little children, had been allowed to accumulate nearly all winter—for otherwise, they would have starved—the husband, an intemperate, shiftless character, died, and the woman was taken away by her friends. But strange to tell, who should be engaged, by and by, as cook in the house of a wealthy family three blocks off, but this very same woman—who grew fat and rosy in a good place, and not only paid the old score, long as it was,—(although Ephraim himself told her it was no matter, and might as well go, now; but the worthy cook began to grow angry then)—not only did she settle the bill, but sent her old friend a deal of profitable custom. The story of his good deeds went to the ears of the mistress, and thence into other people's; and you may depend Ephraim didn't lose anything by that. So with all his soft-heartedness the man might be said to gain nearly enough to balance the really bad accounts; for they were not always coming back, after he gave them up—those unfortunate bills.

This was the sort of personage that the little flax-headed boy was lucky enough to come to. He didn't seem to have performed any morning toilet; he was bare-headed and bare-footed; finally he was about ten years old.

"And who are you, my man?" said Ephraim, for he had never seen the youngster before, although he knew, or thought so, every mother's child for a dozen blocks around.

The tow head looked up in the shopkeeper's face and answered that his usual appellation was Jack.

"And where do you come from?" continued Ephraim.

Master Jack looked up again, but returned no reply at all. He drew in a long breath and let it out again,—that sort of half sigh that children sometimes make: still keeping his eyes at Ephraim's.

"I want some breakfast," boldly came from his lips at last.

Ephraim stopped a moment in his work of hauling out before the door his stands and milk cans; but the bit of astonishment was followed by something very much like gratified vanity. It wouldn't be every man, or woman either, that a little unfortunate, might appeal to with the style of Jack's laconic speech. It was not a style where effrontery or the callous tone of an accustomed beggar struck out. It was rather like saying—sir, I see that you have a good heart, and that it always delights you to do a charitable deed.

There was another thing. Ephraim had, ten months before, been the possessor of a little white head, not much different from Jack's, only a good deal younger. But it was its fate one melancholy evening, to be the subject of the consultation of three doctors of medicine, who attended it for five successive days. At the end of that time the little white head was whiter than ever, for it was dead. So the good fellow's heart, thenceforward, warmed toward children with a still deeper warmth than before.

Without any more ado, or any talk about it, the milkman and the child by silent consent, seemed to form a mental compact.—The new assistant took hold; and the two helped each other in all the preparations and putting to rights. Tow-head sprinkled the flagstones in front, and swept them off; he would have done the same thing to the floor inside—only the owner himself had done it already.

As he bustled and brushed about, Ephraim more than once stopped, under the influence of a meditative abstraction; he probably weighed in his mind the chances of the newcomer's honesty—for he looked closely at him from time to time. What particular notions flitted through the tow-head, I now forget.

And yet I ought to know something about it, for I was myself the forsaken young vagabond, who found a friend in that pearl of a milkman. The spirit of Christ impelled you, Ephraim, whether you knew it or not. If I had been turned off with a surly answer, there might have been a body lost—or perhaps a soul; for I was sorely distressed.—Parentless and homeless—just at the turning point where familiarity with crime is developed into something worse—such was I when you took me in and ministered unto me.

CHAPTER III.

Something for the special consideration of those who pay two hundred a year pew rent, and take the sacrament from vessels of silver and gold: Billjiggs, his life and death: wounds, and balm for the same.

AT THIS TIME, I have only a confused and occasionally distinct recollection of my fortunes previous to the morning at the milkman's.

You have doubtless, supposing you to have lived in or ever visited New-York, seen there many a little vagabond, in dirty tatters and shirtless. They generally wander along in men's boots, picked up somewhere, whose disproportionate size makes it necessary for them to keep their feet sliding along, without lifting from the ground. The shuffling movement thus acquired sometimes sticks to them through life.

Nobody either cares, or appears to care, for these juvenile loafers. Some are the children of shame, and are cast out because they would be a perpetual memento of disgrace to their generators. Some are orphans of the poorest classes. Others run away from parental brutality; which is pretty plentiful, after all, among both high and low. Others again take to the streets for very sustenance; those who should naturally be their protectors living lives of drunkenness and improvidence.

The revelations of the Reports of the Chief of the Police, about this extensive element in what is termed the rising generation, are terrible and romantic in their naked facts, far beyond any romance of the novelist.

What I remember of my life previous to my introduction in the second chapter, was mostly located among this class. We were indeed wanderers upon the face of the earth; although our travels did not extend beyond the limits of the city, and the places within a few miles' distance. The only principle that controlled us was the instinct to live, animally; to eat, (if we could get it,) when we were hungry, and to lie down and sleep wherever weariness overtook us.

I have a very clear recollection of a most intimate crony, with whom I shared luck and adventures; and who did the same with me. He was a little older than myself. His name, he always said, was William, or Bill, Jiggs; but we all used to call him Billjiggs, for convenience.

Billjiggs was quite a magnificent fellow. When elated or very good humored, indeed, he was wont to announce himself as one of the boys you read of in the Scriptures; though which of these numerous worthies he meant, he never specified. He had red hair,—very red. It was never combed; but it was cut every few days, by the friend who happened to be the handiest; sometimes with a scissors, sometimes with a jackknife, sharpened for the work; and once, I remember with a broad-axe. I had the honor of handling the implement myself on that occasion. Some carpenters, at work on a new house, had gone to dinner nearby, and left their tools lying loose around. Poor Billjiggs! I came very near laying his head open.

My friend would never allow me to be imposed upon by superior force or cunning; and though I was too little to add much to his weight in his own quarrels, still I sometimes managed to cast the balance in his favor, in cases where the odds were pretty nearly even. For Billjiggs was pugnacious; he entered into quarrels and fights on the smallest pretence, and sometimes received horrible drubbings.

One day, I remember, he pitched into a boy considerably bigger than himself, for some curt rejoinder to a critical remark of Billjiggs, about a certain spotted cap which the aforesaid boy chose to wear on his head. He of the spotted cap got considerably the worst of the battle, which waxed hot; when he was fain to seize a good-sized paving stone that happened to be loose in the street, and dealt Billjiggs such a blow on the side of his head that he fell flat and senseless on the ground, and the blood poured forth freely; the victor taking to his heels like a good fellow.

I mention this incident because it was the means of my first seeing an individual who years afterward, (as the reader will find in the course of the story,) played a prominent part in the affairs of my life.

Billjiggs was carried in the nearest basement, and restoratives applied to him.

An old Quaker lady, and a little girl of my own age, appeared to be the only ones at home. The old lady was very kind in her manner; and after washing Billjiggs' dirty and bloody head, and applying plasters from the neighboring druggist's, bound it up in her own large, clean, white linen handkerchief. The little girl had to fasten the knot in it, for the old lady's fingers were not nimble enough. She did so very tenderly and neatly; and she seemed to me, as I looked at her, to be a little red-cheeked angel from Heaven.

Billjiggs afterwards kept that handkerchief and couldn't be induced to part with it anyway. He took it with him to Mexico, several years afterward; where the poor fellow met with an uglier wound than that of the paving stone; and no old Quaker lady to look after him; a wound which sent him to a grave among the prickly cactuses.

Such was the end of Billjiggs; than whom there are many worse young men, who dress in clean shirts, with straight high collars, and go to church of a Sunday.

This little girl—the old lady called her Martha—spoke so pleasantly to me, too; and the old lady, when we went away, told me to come there from time to time, and get what she had to bestow, either of food or clothing.

I don't know how it was; but neither I nor my friend ever stepped foot in that basement afterward, even when we were the hungriest. For the first time almost in our lives, we had been treated with rational benevolence, and as if we were real human beings. I know, in my case, it touched me with a feeling I never remembered before. Although I would have died for the old lady, or the child, I felt something like pride toward them; or perhaps for their good opinion.

My impression is to this day, that the little episode I have just described; that gentle old face surrounded with the plain lace edging of its cap, and the silver hair so smoothly folded—and that other face, emblem of purity and infantile goodness—and the glimpse that came upon me, of a happy, peaceful, honest, well-ordered life; my belief is, I say, that all this acted with the influence of a good genius upon me, afterward. Child as I was, (ah, how far more deeply children think, than most people imagine!) I saw something of the moral of the difference between the meanness and poverty and degradation of my class, and the delicacy and wholesomeness and safety of that Quaker family. I knew that I was of the same flesh and blood, and the same nature, as they. I was encouraged, and ah how much more benefited by their really respectful kindness, than they dreamed of!

And here is a consideration, that the theorist on the evils of society might build a big structure upon; but as I am only jotting down a story of incidents, I will leave whoever sees these paragraphs, to carry out the train of thought for himself.

CHAPTER IV.

A hint for unsuccessful schoolmasters and parents; the first woman with whom I fell in love; my teens, and how they went; I make a beginning at the big cheese; which leads to a dinner for three.

WHATEVER SEEDS of evil and degradation my life in the streets had infused in my character, before I took up my abode with Ephraim Foster, had no chance to grow afterward. Both his wife and himself treated me like a son; and better than many people treat their sons. Kindness choked out all lingering tendencies to mischief within me; and the sentiment which just flickered a moment in my mind, when we were in the basement of the Quaker lady's house, here grew into form and permanence; and I loved that rough husk of a fellow with a love which was only overtopped by my affection for my dear mother, (as I always call her) his wife Violet.

Violet! That was the name of one for whom I bear a sentiment imperishable until my heart perishes!

Let me describe her.

This woman with the name of a frail and humble flow had the bodily height and breadth, of a good-sized ma. She was a country girl, when Ephraim married her, and loved to work out-doors. Her features were coarse; only her complexion was clean and healthy; and her eyes beamed with perpetual cheerfulness, and willingness to oblige. She had little education and what is called in the hot-house taste of the present day, intellect. She had no more idea of what are now called Woman's Rights, than of the sublimest wonders of geology. But she had a beautiful soul; and her coarse big features were lighted up with more sweetness, to me, than any Madonna of Italian masters.

With the strength of a horse, Violet possessed the gentleness of a dove. How sweetly tasted the first food she prepared for me; how fresh and fragrant the homely clothes, I was given to put on that morning, after a bath in a big tub in the woodhouse; and how kindly the tone in which I was reminded of observances about the place, that day. For Violet was a critical housekeeper, and dirt was an abomination in her eyes.

Patient, considerate, self-denying, Mother! Blessed is the home, blessed are the children, where such as you are found.

Nearly ten years of my life were here passed, smoothly and happily. A great portion of the last six, was spent at school; although I often wished to stop that, and undertake some trade, or employment; but my parents would not have it so. They prospered fairly: and said that they made a decent living enough now, and it would perhaps be my turn by and by, when they grew old.

Ephraim had his mind set on my following the profession of the law. I did not steadily oppose him in this, after I found out it was a darling notion; but the truth was, it by no means agreed with my own fancy.

The brightest jewel, saith the Persian poet, that glitters on the neck of the young man is the spirit of adventure. I felt this spirit within me; but I repressed it, and made it dumb, for I regarded their feeling who had lifted me into life, worthy to be so called.

You already know of my introduction to the lawyer Covert. I went the next day according to appointment, and made a beginning. This consisted simply in my master's giving me an outline of the course of primary reading for a law student; and in my getting familiar with the office, just to take the rawness off.

I was much amused with Nathaniel, the office-boy, and felt a sincere pity for old Wigglesworth; and before the morning passed away we three were on very good terms together. Nat was pert enough, but he had a fund of real wit of which he was sufficiently lavish, in season, and out of season. He saluted me with gravity as "Don Cesar de Bazan;" from a resemblance he assumed to discover between myself and the player of that part at the theatre which Nathaniel was in the habit of honoring with an occasional shilling, and his presence. And Don Cesar he persisted in calling me from that time.

"Let not my lord forget that the banquet waits," said this precious youth with a droll obeisance.

It was half-past 12, and I was to treat to a cheap dinner that day, in commemoration of the important era of my career.

We knew that Mr. Covert had an appointment to meet some clients at this time, and, (as Wigglesworth told me very often happened,) he signified his wish for a clear kitchen.

The parties just anticipated our departure. Two ladies came in a carriage, which we saw at the door; a big black driver, dressed in a cape surtout, seated on the box.

These ladies, (this Wigglesworth also told me in the street) were the wealthy Madam Seligny and her daughter. Madam was fat enough, and red enough; had a hooked nose, and keen black eyes. Her person glistened and rustled with jewelry and silks, diffusing a strong scent of musk, with every movement. She had a yellow silk bonnet, set back on her head; and her fat hands gloved in white kid, applied a perfumed handkerchief of costly lace, to the before-mentioned nose. She waddled, rather than walked, and sank down panting in the great chair which Mr. Covert had placed for her.

Rebecca, the daughter, offered mettle more attractive. She was a pretty good specimen of Israelitish beauty, tall and slender, and in the full maturity of womanhood. She dressed with some taste, although richly, and with a little of her national fondness for jewelry.

Going downstairs, I was aware that Mr. Covert, from the inside, shut the door and locked it.

Our dinner was eaten, with much approval, and not a little mirth. We had some sparkling cider, which Nathaniel declared made him feel quite young again. Wigglesworth brightened up too, and offered a toast wishing that I might have the very best luck the law could offer.

"That," said Nat, "would be to hold on where you are, and never put your foot in Covert's office again. For if you want to know this child's opinion about him, it is just—"

But the boy stopped himself suddenly, and in a few moments we adjourned.

In the next chapter I shall fill up the blank Nat left; and also tell how I got along at the law.

CHAPTER V.

A young man in a perplexing predicament; some philosophy about the same; Nathaniel and his dog; I behold a young lady, under circumstances that try her temper.

COULD I STAND IT? Would it not turn my young blood into something of a molasses article—something to be gauged and weighed, involving tare and tret, and the sage confabulations of those solid, bald-headed, respectable old gentlemen, with pencils in one hand, and little blank books in the other? Could such an eternal procession of chapter ones, title twos, and section threes, have any other result than to make my brain revolve like this earth, on its own axis? Would it not be better to settle the difficulty with courage, by calling a council of Ephraim Foster, Violet and Covert, and frankly telling them that I found I was neither fitted for the study of the law, nor the study of the law for me; and kindly but resolutely declare my determination to go no further?

I had been five weeks a student, in Covert's office, and the preceding reflections were the result.

At my age—I have before mentioned that I was just past twenty—a young man of intelligence and health, wants something to engross him—some real object, for his vitality, his feelings, his almost boundless moral and physical spring. It is indefinite what it should be; some find that object in the gratification of an eager desire to go to sea, to visit different places, or other methods of mere change of locality. Some get it in the pursuit of a particular aim, on which they have set their hearts; these aims are as various as mankind, only the pursuit must not be shut out to them.

With me, this craving could never be satisfied with the study of law. That was becoming more and more repugnant to me. I had not yet tasted very deeply, it is true, but it was quite enough. I felt one of those strong presentiments that I could not be happy in that way—one of those instincts which, without arguing much on the subject, it is generally wise to follow.

But then my good father—the man who had saved me from ruin—who had overwhelmed me with obligations—who even now supplied me more liberally with pocket money, than many rich men do their sons—and whose heart was firmly set on this very thing!

One time lately, in a manner which would admit the inference of either joke or earnest, I had ventured a few words, for an experiment, to see how Ephraim would look on any such move as turning a short corner in my studentship. His countenance fell, and he winced like a fellow under a shower bath.

Could I so thoroughly displease this man, in almost the only serious point where he had demanded from me a compliance with his will? Allowing that it were a penance to me, ought I not to submit, even for his sake, if for no other? And would not time change my aversion, and perhaps make me ashamed of my childish prejudices and weakness?

Such debates and contradictions worried me exceedingly; causing my commencement in Covert's office, and the following few weeks, to make a real blotch in my usually happy fortunes. And after all I came to no decision. I waded on through the slough of Chapters, titles and sections, as before; and began, I fancied, to look pale and thin, as indeed became a professional personage.

Not but that the dryness and cloudiness of my occupation were often relieved by gleams of warmth, interest or fun. It was impossible not to be amused with Master Nat, and nearly all his sayings and doings, including his attachment to, and the tricks he taught, his big, docile dog Jack, whose capers, sagacity, and even his expressive look, and long yellow wool, were the delight of the boy's life. Never was brute more thought of than Jack, by Nathaniel; and he returned his master's friendship in kind.

Jack, indeed, was very free in his demonstrations. This was exhibited one afternoon, when he and Nathaniel returned from dinner. In the office, by the table, stood a lady, while at his desk in the next room Mr. Covert held serious talk with Pepperich Ferris, a stock and financial speculator, who frequently came there on business.

The lady, who was young yet, although old enough to have cut her wisdom teeth, appeared to be waiting for Ferris. She had the stylish, self-possessed look, which sometimes marks those who follow a theatrical life. Her face, though not beautiful, was open and pleasing, with bright black eyes, and a brown complexion. Her figure, of good height and graceful movement, was dressed in a costly pale colored silk.

"Ah, you have a beautiful dog," said she, as Jack marched up to her, wagging his tail. And she leaned to pat him on the head and shoulders.

Jack gave up his heart without delay, and, in an instant, two large and particularly muddy paws were planted on the folds of the pale silk.

The lady uttered a slight scream, and started indignantly back; for she was but woman, and the dress was truly splendid. But when Mr. Covert came forward in great anger, and chid Nathaniel severely, and reminded him of former prohibitions about bringing Jack upon those sacred premises—and when the sagacious brute crawled in a by-place, with evidently depressed spirits—and Nathaniel was more chop-fallen than would be supposed for that philosophic young gentleman—then the lady laughed a good-natured laugh.

"Oh, it is nothing," she said. "It is nothing. It was my own fault, for I called him."

And she snapped her fingers and called Jack again; and expressed her confidence in the spots washing off without the least trouble; and insisted that the lawyer should find no more fault with the boy, to whom she herself spoke pleasantly.

The consequence of which was a few days afterwards, that I, at Nathaniel's suggestion, incurred an expense of some five dollars, and went to the theatre on a benefit night, after giving Wigglesworth a ticket, besides similar gifts of the same sort to one or two boys, Nathaniel's sworn cronies.

CHAPTER VI.

The dancing girl on a benefit night: I introduce the reader to the valuable acquaintance of J. Fitzmore Smytthe.

UPON THE STAGE she looked really fascinating, and her pale silk dress, with those great folds which the dog spoiled, had given place to the short gauzy costume of a dancing girl. Her legs and feet were beautiful, and her gestures and attitudes easy and graceful, to a degree hardly ever seen among the mechanical performers of the ballet.

When this fine looking girl—this Inez—came forward in her part, I heard a specially clattering applause, over in a corner of the house, where, upon examination, I discovered Master Nathaniel, and his friends, each armed with big sticks, which they plied vigorously upon all the wooden work in their neighborhood.

New York is a progressive city, of vast resources; but in nothing is its energy more perceptible than in its juvenile population proper—their culture and their beginning early.

From Nathaniel and his friends, my attention was now attracted nearer by.

"Um—m—m; devilish lovely girl. Um—m—m. Ah?"

Such was the remark of a fashionably attired gentleman by my side, who nodded approvingly toward me. I had a slight acquaintance with him, and had fallen foul of him, that evening, just on entering the theatre, where we happened to take seats together. He was clerk in a bank not far from Covert's office, and the name on his very genteel little enamelled card, was "J. Fitzmore Smytthe."

Really I beg pardon all round for not introducing, with specific description, long before, this same Fitzmore Smytthe. Our acquaintance was, in fact, one that dated back some seasons beforehand. He was only four or five years my elder; and I first knew him as the assistant of a small dry-goods store, in the neighborhood of our house. Young Mr. Smytthe even then, although but a boy, was very, very genteel. Conversational powers he had acquired only on a solitary theme, that of selling dry-goods to the ladies—he on one side of the counter, they on the other. These powers were, however, somewhat brilliant in that way. They might be illustrated or summed up in the following phrases, varied to suit any difference of the rank, age, or temperament, of purchasers.

"Shall I show you anything else to-day, ma'am?"

"No ma'am, we haven't any of that article; it's not worn at all, now."

"Where will you have these things sent, ladies?"

"This is real French goods, ma'am, and is very much worn.—I will put it to you low."

"Ah, that would be lower than cost price, ma'am."

"Indeed, I am sure you will be pleased with it.—I warrant it to wash like a rock."

"This will be somewhat dearer, ma'am; it is the very best material, and one-and-threepence is positively the lowest I could afford it."

&c, &c, &c, &c.

Take Fitzmore on any other tack, and he floundered like a whale in the shallows.—He retreated to a dull muttering, interspersed with an occasional spasm of meaning.—This muttering, or mumble, had the great advantage of leaving the hearer to make out of it any sort of sentiment, which said hearer chose to infer.—This was often very convenient.

"Um—m—;" "Ah, I believe so;" and phrases of that sort, made up most of my friend's stock, now that he was out of the dry-goods line.

In response to his praise of the dancing girl, I asked him if he had seen her before.

"Um—m—m—Should think so—Devilish intimate with Inez—Visit her."

I knew that Smytthe had an ambition to be on familiar terms with all sorts of notabilities; and, as the dance was over we walked out, and into a neighboring refreshment saloon, where he told me what he knew of Inez.

She was Spanish by birth, but must have been, from early life in England; at any rate, she talked the language without any foreign tone. She was very independent, had the reputation of possessing some money, well invested;

and although much talked about, Smytthe averred that she was as good as other people; and only to a few, of which he broadly hinted that he was one, deigned the favor of her smiles and her friendship. He announced to me quite confidentially, that he often visited her, and that they were on the best terms in the world together.

Probably he read something like incredulity in my looks, for, warming over his glass of wine, he promised me, if I wished it, to give me an opportunity of paying the charming Spaniard a visit, one evening, in his company.

CHAPTER VII.

Portrait of a black sheep: how the lawyer cheated the carpenter: my acquaintance with Inez ripens marvellously.

THE CHARACTER of Covert did not take me long to understand, particularly as Wigglesworth volunteered a good deal of information about him; and what I could not help seeing from day to day in the office, made up the rest. That he was an unprincipled man, with boundless selfishness and avarice, seemed sure enough; but whether he was a cunning villain, or no, puzzled me to tell.

Covert, from what I had learned of Wigglesworth, had come reasonably by his swindling disposition. His father had given him lessons in it early, and he proved an apt scholar. One of his first tricks, when, as a young man, he entered upon the practice of the law, was as follows—the two arranging a plan to this effect. The father entered into a contract with an honest carpenter, who had got about enough ahead for him to take such a speculation, to build a house. The plan was decided on, the terms fixed, the papers drawn out, a day being mentioned in them with rigid conditions on which the house was to be completed—and the carpenter undertook his work. He had credit with the lumber, hardware, and other dealers; for he already possessed some little property of his own, and he hoped to satisfy a mortgage upon that, with the profits he should make out of Covert's job; for he did a good deal of the work himself. He had a numerous family, and he was very anxious to have for them a permanent home.

Well, the job went on swimmingly; the house being enclosed, and a great portion of the inside work done. But as it went on, the Coverts discovered that they wanted additional improvements made inside—various fine finishings, cornices, and etceteras, which could only be done slowly. The carpenter told the elder Covert that, in that way, the house could not be finished at the time specified; the answer was, (no one else being by,) not to mind, but to go on and do the work well, without troubling about the particular day it should be completed.

Our carpenter was unsuspicious, and he took the matter very easily, until the arrival of the period mentioned in the contract.—The next day as he was at work in the house with his apprentices and journeymen, he was quite thunderstruck by the coming of two constables, who ordered the premises to be cleared, and then closed and nailed them up!

The two scoundrels had taken their precautions, and prepared their way, but too well; they had the law on their side, and the mechanic and his family were ruined.—For a trumpery claim of damages was established, and not a single dollar did Covert pay for the work. The lumber and hardware merchants levied for their bills, on the carpenter's own little property, all of which it took to pay them, and every dollar of his toil-earned savings was at once swept away.

Such formed one of Lawyer Covert's beginnings in life, under the tutoring of his precious parent—who was withal a sanctified man, wore a white neckcloth, and wouldn't have taken the name of the Lord in vain, on any account. Whether the old fellow is alive yet I don't know; but the son is—damn him!

Covert—of course I am talking of the lawyer, now—had, among the forms of his selfishness, some political ambition. He had been up once already, for the State Legislature, but was defeated. At the present time he took some pains to get a nomination for the Assembly; our city members being then elected by general ticket, and he expected to be carried on the tide with the rest, for his party had shown a handsome working majority, as it is called, at the preceding contest.

Wigglesworth could not say much about Covert's pecuniary condition. He told me that the lawyer lived in good style, however, in an up-town street; that, although occasionally pinched for money, he managed to make both ends meet; and that his business was tolerably extensive.

In his treatment of me the lawyer was civil, without paying any particular attention. He evidently didn't consider me worth taking much pains about, either to gain my friendship, or prevent my enmity; and doubtless troubled his mind little concerning me. It looked business-like to have a student in the office, and I was occasionally of some assistance in copying, or hunting up authorities.

All this while my dislike to the profession remained the same, and the conflict was from time to time resumed, in my mind, whether to give it up or not. Covert himself was such an unfavorable illustration of the class, that it by no means helped to reconcile me to the prospect of joining them.

Inez visited our office two or three times after the adventure with Jack; and, somehow, we struck up quite an acquaintance together. I must confess I was a little bashful at first, but her manner was easy and sociable without being at all forward; and a young man does not long remain bashful when treated kindly by a pretty woman.

One day Inez had to wait half an hour, for Mr. Covert's return. Old Wigglesworth sat in his corner, deeply immersed in some specially intricate copying; Nathaniel was out in the long wide passage-way, having a romp with his dog; and, as no one else seemed on hand to do the honors, I placed a chair for Inez, sat down nearby on another, and soon made quite astonishing progress, for a youth who knew so little of the sex. We talked, laughed, spoke of Inez' benefit, and so forth; and had a very agreeable hour, toward the close of which the Spaniard gave me her address, and invited me to call and see her, as she was not to perform that evening.

I mentioned Mr. J. Fitzmore Smytthe's name, and said that he spoke of her as an old acquaintance. She laughed and said, "Bring him along with you; for I don't know that I dare have you come and see me alone."

Now it struck me that I had a great deal rather not have him, and I told Inez so; but she laughed more heartily than before.

"I make Smytthe an indispensable condition," said she, "for I see that my fears were well founded."

Covert now came in, and our sociability, much to my regret, was done with.

From the conversation that ensued, for I was curious to know what brought her here, I found that these visits of the dancing girl had reference to some investment of her spare funds in stock. Covert, among his other employments, had got himself chosen officer in an insurance company; and Pepperich Ferris and Smytthe were instrumental in advising Inez to make the investment. Perhaps I had no ground for suspicion, yet I determined to find out something of the particulars of the affair; for I didn't consider either Smytthe or Ferris immaculate.

CHAPTER VIII.

The character and home of the Dancing Girl— A delightful evening, for three—I almost fall in love, if jealousy is any sign.

INEZ—SHE NEVER went by any other name, except in legal documents, when the term, 'a Spanish dancing girl,' was added; Inez belonged to that class of professional people, including a majority of those whose parents earn their living, by serving the public, and depending on the latter's favor, who are prematurely developed.

These unfortunates have the experience of men and women while yet in early youth. Under feverish stimulants, they come forward, like hot-house plants, and sometimes their growth is unwholesome, and as fragile.

With Inez, however, there was the saving fact of a strong vein of native common sense. She afterward told me, when we became more intimate, that the first man she really loved, (and she loved in the morning of her life,) taught her the most profitable lesson she had ever learned. He was treacherous; she was devoted and confiding. And that treachery it was that with the scorching mark of a hot iron, burnt on her heart, the precept *Caution*, the great need that is so long coming to young souls, and that, when it comes, puts an end forever to the freshest joys, and the thoughtless abandon, of their lives. And yet it is so useful in this wicked world; and we cannot get along without it. And so, as the dose must be taken, the sooner the wry face is past, and the qualms gone, the better.

"Oh," said the frank-hearted girl, "I have not traveled alone through so many lands; I have not gained my bread, among shows, and coarse people—making journeys, and taking up with any kind of accommodation—subject to all sorts of proposals, and all variations of applause, indifference, and scorn: I have not gone through these, and much more, for nothing.

"You have candidly asked me my own opinion of myself. I will be as candid with you. I know that I am not good. But I feel also that I never have been, and am not, abandoned enough to be unworthy the sympathy of those who are good. I am conscious of having committed no spiteful meanness; I wound or deceive no one who trusts in me. I have never wronged a human being—I have not thought myself better than the degraded and lost ones—but rather pity and relieve them."

She stopped abruptly, and looked at us with her sharp black eyes.

"But am I not making myself ridiculous?" she added.

On the contrary, I felt a real admiration for this independent and, in some respects, unfortunate girl; and the evident truth which impelled her to talk of her character in that way, impressed my feelings strongly.

But—whether jealousy or not, something put the thought in my head at this moment—could this woman love such a fop as Smytthe? She might have got along with Smytthe, because that is a manly acceptance of one's destiny, and a plump defiance of the world. But in Smytthe, was a sort of sneaking and cowardly evasion—a consciousness of something wrong, and a timid desire to dust people's eyes about it.

I answered nothing to the question of Inez, and Smytthe gave his eternal

"Ah—O—um—um—m—O, no indeed."

We had coffee, and some biscuits. It was delightful coffee, made by Inez herself, in, as she told us, the Spanish fashion.

A stout, rosy, Irish woman—of all people in the world, Mrs. Nancy Fox, wife of Barney Fox, and mother of seven little Foxes—served us these refreshments. Or rather she appeared to serve us, but Inez was in such good spirits and so nimble and graceful, that she really did everything.

Barney and Nancy and the little children, lived in a rear building on the same premises, and the services of the tidy industrious Irish woman, were quite invaluable to Inez, who had formed an attachment to her, and requited her liberally. Barney followed the honorable business of hod-carrying, and at a pinch, even took a place under government, as a street-sweeper. Barney was up to snuff, too, as will be shown by and by.

And now, when I look back upon it, there have been stupider evenings passed, than the one which was talked and sipped away by us in that comfortable little parlor. There we were in easy chairs encompassing a round table in the middle of the room; a fine astral lamp shedding a soft light over everything; the cheerful fire, for it was a chilly evening, in the open grate—by the side whereof, on a substantial ottoman, when everybody had been helped to coffee—was placed Mrs. Fox herself, in her snowy cap and clean check apron—placed there compulsorily and as well supplied as the rest, by Inez herself, with one of the junior Foxes, pretty little Maggy, crouching close into the folds of her gown, and quite too much awe-struck with the grandeur of the scene, to enjoy the cakes which Inez fed her with from time to time.

By Jupiter! yes. I remember it so well, now. Inez brought out an old guitar, the tuning whereof was a work of more labor than love. She sang to us some pleasing songs—first in English, and then, as the evening wore on, and she sang better, in Spanish. And when Mrs. Fox, burthened with the fragments of the feast—quite a stock of delicacies for her—took her departure, we sat and listened, and listened.

Inez had not a voice of much power; but there was deep feeling in her songs, and in her way of performing them. They were plaintive, without being melancholy.

The night was by no means extremely late when we left. Somewhat to my surprise and far more to my gratification, my quondam friend Smytthe departed with me.

"Why," said I, as he took his hat, and went forth into the passageway, at the same time, "Why I supposed you were to stay——that is, I didn't know you were going with me now."

I no sooner uttered the words than I felt that I had made an unfortunate slip. Smytthe colored and twirled his little whisker.

"Um-m-m, not at present, I think."

Inez darted her keen eyesight from his face to mine. Doubtless with woman's intuition she divined the real truth.

There was a pause, for a moment, and I felt a little apprehensive that the hot-blooded Spaniard was going to give us a taste of her temper.

But she didn't. She laughed gaily, and then with more deliberation than usual she said, looking me in the face,

"Of all supposings in the world, you could not have supposed anything more absurd. You will learn that to a certainty, one of these days; for I hope you will come and see me again when I send for you—for we have had a pleasant evening, and I like you: Good night. Good night, Smytthe."

And she quickly turned, went in, and locked the door, without waiting for another word.

“Um-m-m,” said the bank clerk, as we walked homeward, “devilish girl for joking. How well she carried off that last one.”

I had never before heard anything from Smytthe involving such a deep process of thought as this way of getting over that dash of cold water.

CHAPTER IX.

Visit Covert's house—Meet there with a person I know and don't know—Two political parties illustrated—Curiosity of Barney Fox.

COVERT SUCCEEDED in getting the nomination; and afterwards there were two or three informal gatherings at his house, to take measures for securing his election. By his request, I was present at one of these; for, since his nomination, he had of course grown very polite—to me among the rest. He wanted Ephraim Foster's vote and influence, which was not small; and, for those meetings, it was his object to have them pretty full.

When I knocked at Covert's door it was just after dark. I found I had anticipated the time, and the lawyer was not yet home. In answer to my pull at the bell a young woman opened the door; and the light of a street lamp falling on her face, reminded me, as people are often vaguely and provokingly reminded, of features they have seen before; but where or how they cannot tell.

The young woman was neatly dressed in Quaker style,

though with warmer colors and a little more of the ornamental than is common in that rigid sect. What the lamplight allowed me to see of her face, impressed me very agreeably. She asked me in, said that Mr. Covert would doubtless be home in a little while, and, if I wished to wait, I could walk in the room. I would wait; but I sat down by a table in the wide hall, on which there were books and newspapers.

The young woman stopped a moment to raise the light that hung suspended from the ceiling; and as she did so, and her face was turned upward, the puzzle of having seen her somewhere, again bothered me. Where could it have been? I was almost tempted to say as much to her; but she had arranged the lamp, and walked quietly down the basement stairs.

Probably Covert's daughter, thought I; and, if so, I could not congratulate her on her parentage. But no; she hadn't any of his features. Her eyes were grey, with a tender, affectionate expression; her face blooming and healthy; her figure plump almost to the point of being fat; and her figure, hands, neck, and so on, all finely formed. Besides, she was very nimble in her movements, with all her plumpness; as I saw, by her management of the lamp, and her walk past me, to the head of the stairs, I even listened, to satisfy myself of the lightness and rapidity of her step.

You see I had arrived, of late, at quite a degree of interest in all these important matters. Particularly since my acquaintance with Inez, I found myself worked up to an astonishing amount of curiosity that way.

When Covert came, he brought a couple of friends with him and we adjourned to the parlor—more people dropped in, and the room was quite full. The two friends were Alderman Rye, an opulent wholesale grocer, and the Hon. Isaac Leech, a gentleman of fortune. Although these were alike supporters of Mr. Covert, they were as far as the poles asunder in their political principles. Principles! Yes; that is what they called them.

"Why, sir," I heard Alderman Rye's voice above the rest, "is not this evidence enough of the poisonous consequences of Whig misrule? Isn't the country already almost ruined—ruined, sir?"

Fortunately I was seated in the back-room, but I heard those shrill voices in front there, quite plainly enough.

"That we are down, sir—that we are down, as a commercial people, I grant you," was the response of the Hon. Isaac Leech, "but not from anything done by the Whig party. Sir, that party is the palladium of our freedom. Sir, the Locofocos would utterly destroy this nation in five years, if they had their own way. Their leaders are blind to truth, and the whole party is regardless of law."

"Law! the Whigs ride over the constitution, without mercy. Bargains, corruption, is their game."

"Did not Gen. Jackson remove those deposits without the shadow of legal authority?"

"But who spent money like water in bribing members of Congress?"

"The veto power, sir, is dangerous to our liberties."

Then a medley of "bargain and corruption," "Clay," "Adams," "I deny it, sir," "I can prove it," and so forth, and so on.

A pretty fair sample, this, of what happened whenever the Hon. Isaac Leech came in contact with Alderman Rye; they seemed not only to enjoy it, but to think they were holding a very profound discussion, of much interest to their hearers.

Covert had some difficulty in choking off these angry disputes, and in broaching the object of the meeting. That was, to make some movement which should carry abroad the appearance of his being popular with both parties. There was a probability of some discontent among the regulars; and he had a hope of getting a good many votes on the opposition side.

I did not stay to take part in it, but departed, after asking Covert if there was any thing he wanted me to do for him.

He pulled out of his pocket a greasy letter, much creased in what appeared to have been unsatisfactory efforts to fold it, and said that he had a good deal to attend to, and it would oblige him if I would answer that—he cared not particularly in what way, except that he wished not to offend the writer of the epistle, and his friends.

"For," said he, "all their votes count, either against me, or for me."

The next morning, I had the pleasure of entering into a correspondence with the gentleman whose name was signed to the fellow's epistle. My first impulse was to decline the job in disgust, but upon second thought I went into the thing as a good joke.

"Sur:—Axin your pardon, I make bold to rite a few lines, bein appinted by a committee of fellow-citizens, for the purpose of informin myself on a few subjecks consarnin the next eleckshun, of which you are a candydate; that is to say, as follose:

What is your opinyun of de street-sweepin masheens?

Are you in favur of rasin sweeper's wages to ten shillings a day?

Will you pledge yourself to vote for a law furnishin sweepers wid a new broom, gratis, for nothin?

Are you in favor of rainy days bein paid for, and men not made to work out in the nasty mud, to the deanger of their hellth?

Sur, many of your fellow-sitizens is deeply interested in your opinyunns on these vitally important subjecks.

Please inform us of your vus on these subjecks at an urly day.

Wid grate respeck,

On behalf of de Committea,

BARNEY FOX."

CHAPTER X.

What different luck the election brought to the lawyer and the street sweeper. I make another visit to Inez.

SOME MONTHS now passed away, carrying with them the fall and winter, during which no incidents occurred, that are necessary to be narrated, in any detailed manner in this veracious history of my life and adventures.

Whether from the unsatisfactory nature of my answer to Barney Fox's questions, or some other cause, Covert lost his election. There had come a revulsion in what the newspapers call public sentiment, and the party which carried the day a season or two before, was now completely swamped. The Hon. Isaac Leech came forth in colors of resplendent glory, and Alderman Rye labored under deep depression of spirits. As to Mr. Fox, he showed more sense than I had given him credit for. He discovered suddenly that he had always been an ardent advocate and laborer for the party now successful; and, on the strength of the importance given him by his appointment as a "committee of one," in an exciting election contest, and as the representative of a large body of fellow-citizens, all of whom have votes, and, like wide-awake members of a republican government ought to do, lose no occasion of using them. Mr. Barney Fox, the cunning dog, before anybody knew it, had the coolness to propose for and secure a really nice little contract for digging out and filling up certain public grounds in his ward!

Now Barney possessed not ten dollars in the world, and his getting the contract was partly the result of his natural impudence, and partly luck. But Barney found friends after his good fortune once came upon him, and from that day was totally oblivious toward street-sweeping, nor took any more interest in "masheens" that might interfere with the manual performance of that avocation. In a few months from the time of his promotion, he bought a big lot of ground at Hoboken, and had a neat comfortable two-story cottage on the same, and moved over Mrs. Fox and the little Foxes, now increased in number to eight; and let out two rooms in the upper story to whoever wanted fine airy lodgings for the summer.

"And a happy woman I'd be this day," said Barney's wife, as she took her departure from the rear building, "if it wasn't for the leavin' of you, Miss Inez. If you were me own daughter, I could not feel sorrier."

"Nancy, dear, you are a good creature, and don't talk about it. For isn't the ferry handy; and shan't I take your two rooms for my own sweet self, this summer, and live with you again?"

This assurance of Inez comforted the good, faithful Irishwoman, more than anything else. She went off, followed by her juvenile procession, all as clean and neat as plenty of soap and pure water could make both their clothes and their bodies. Nancy was the tidiest dame in the land, and a good looking one withal, and Inez, as I have before intimated, had a thoroughly filial affection for her. She had bestowed a hearty kiss and a present besides on every little Fox, before the procession took its departure.

Inez gave me this description the same evening, when I visited her, really for my own good pleasure, but nominally to beg permission to bring a friend who had seen her on the stage, and was eager for a closer acquaintance. It was a ridiculous whim, so I thought it anyhow, for Inez to insist so generally on my paying visits only when accompanied by a companion. Our acquaintance had now continued several months, and this was about the first time, whenever I came without Smytthe, or when Nancy was away minding her brood of children, that she did not, under some trivial pretence or other, either shorten her own stay in the room, or frankly say,

"Now, there's a good boy, don't stay any longer, for I want to be alone. Don't take any offence, only I want you to go."

It was cool, but her manner was so good-natured, and there was no help for it.

This evening I was more fortunate. The Spaniard was in her most pleasant humor, and I fell into giving her a description of my early vagabond life, which proved to be, as we soon discovered on comparing notes, not unlike her own in some respects.

"And have you really the singular fortune," asked the dancing girl, "not to know who your parents were?"

"I have that singular fortune, good or bad, whichever it may be," returned I.

Inez favored me with a glance of sympathy.

"Unless Old Wigglesworth is going to tell me all about it," I added, laughing, "for he gave out some strange hints the other day, and seemed to be on the point of imparting to me a terrible secret. Poor old fellow!—You know him, do you not?"

"The little toothless old man, always writing in the corner of your office?"

"That's Mr. Wigglesworth; a gentleman for many years fond of brandy or gin, as came most convenient. Of late, under the ministerings of Mr. Calvin Peterson—father of the young man who, as I was telling you, wishes the pleasure of your valuable acquaintance—under his ministerings poor Wigglesworth has become a Methodist, of the most devoted sort—indeed a real prostrate and convicted sinner, who thinks only of the world to come."

"Poor old man," said Inez, "don't make fun of him. No doubt he is better than either of us."

"No doubt, I think so too, my beautiful Inez; but we are

not old nor toothless, and there is a great deal of heavenly enjoyment in the world that quite attracts my attention from anything in the world to some."

I took the liberty of looking at Inez in a manner which brought me the reward of a boxed ear; and the dancing girl, blushing but laughing, went and sat on the other side of the table.

This evening I certainly felt my first instalment of the cunning of the devil, which might be expected to come in due time to one who persisted in studying the profession of the law. I turned the conversation to my early life again; for that was a sort of connecting link between Inez and myself, in sympathy as well as fact. I saw that she was interested, and that, as I went jabbering on with my narration, the glow of interest and pity colored her face. I thought, before, that she looked well; but now she seemed bewitching. The blood rushed like race horses through my young veins.

The hours wore on, for, somehow, our tongues were loosed, and we both had more to tell, interesting egotists that we were, than seemed possible to be condensed into one night. Inez spoke of her own childhood; but she had parents, and that was a great advantage. The advantage, though, did not continue long, for her parents died while she was yet very young; and afterward it was that came her toughest time of existence. It was indeed full of pitfalls and just-escaped quicksands. She narrated her life with great candor, and an impassioned fluency gave her a peculiar charm.

I know not how it was, but before we were aware of it, we were seated close to one another again, and my hand fell upon her white shoulder, sending an electric shock through my whole frame. Inez was more charitable now, and my ears escaped this time:

Yes, our early lives had been not unlike. My voice sank to a low tone, for Inez was quite near enough to hear me; and I spoke of those days and scenes of wandering and hunger and misery. My poor friend Billjiggs was not forgotten; and it pleased the generous hearted Spaniard right well to hear of his rude courage and self-denial, and the protection he wielded in my behalf.

I spoke of Ephraim Foster, too, and the good Violet. They, above all, were after Inez' own heart, and there was a pressure on my arm responsively to the eloquent description, as I'm sure it was, which I gave of their kindness to me; and to the blessings I called down upon them. I grew more and more pliant of tongue, and recalled for the dancing girl, who had not for some time spoken a word, the impression she first made upon me, when I saw her at Covert's office, at the time the dog planted his muddy paws on her dress. I expatiated on our pleasant acquaintanceship since; and as in a voice lower still, I spoke of the hearts beating against each other, of two young living and loving beings, I pressed a burning kiss upon her lips.

CHAPTER XI.

Questions which seemed no chance of being answered.—
My name accounted for—Calvin Peterson, and
his boarder—Curiosity of Covert.

WIGGLESWORTH WAS certainly a little demented.

"How do you know your name ought to be Jack Engle? It's right, of course—O, of course. But why don't you inquire? Inquire of whom? Who knows? Perhaps I know; perhaps Covert knows; perhaps Ephraim Foster knows."

These were some of the sagacious remarks of Wigglesworth, jerked out now and then, when no one was in the office but we two. Since his conversion to Methodism, the old man had altogether given up drinking, and the result was, that without the stimulant which had been his accustomed support for fifty years, he felt low spirited enough at times. He looked worse than ever; and, after taking the advice of Ephraim, I counselled the old man to indulge himself moderately in drinking. For it was now too late; Wigglesworth stood with one foot in the grave, and, to deprive him totally of drink, we thought likely, under the circumstances, to do him more harm than good. If he had reformed in that respect years before, however, he would no doubt have now been a healthier and a happier man.

With respect to my name being what appears at the head of this auto-biography, all that I knew about it was this—for Ephraim and Violet had informed me of as much, and it tallied with my own recollection:

Jack Engle was the name whereby I called myself, and remembered being called among the very few who use more than my first appellative; it was the name which I gave at our first acquaintance to Violet's serious questionings. Moreover, the morning I came, in my rags, to the benevolent milkman's door, I was wearing in my ear a ring, some three-quarters of an inch in diameter, which I never remembered being put there, but which I knew had hung there as long as my childish memory could know anything about it. It was a plain round ring, with a thick square bar straight across the lower quarter; and somehow had stuck to me through all my wanderings. Probably this good luck was attributable to the fact that the ring, in its dimness and dirt, passed for nothing more valuable than brass.

Upon an examination which Violet made, soon after their adoption of me, this ring proved to be of gold. The little cross bar was double, and when the two parts were separated, there was plainly to be seen, on the one which was concealed before, the words "Jack Engle"; a discovery which so confirmed my juvenile traditions that Ephraim and his wife concluded to give up their first intention of bestowing upon me their own name. Besides, they had some honest religious scruples about their right to make any change. Who knew but what I had been christened with that name?

A year afterward an incident occurred which, although perhaps of no importance, may as well be mentioned here; for it was one of the very few links which had any connection with the mystery of who the deuce I was, and whence I came.

Our pious acquaintance, once casually alluded to in the last chapter, Mr. Calvin Peterson, eked out a frequently scanty living by taking boarders. Calvin wouldn't have any but pious ones; and his accommodations were not very select.

One of his inmates—perhaps two years subsequent to the period described in the second chapter, where I do myself the honor of making the reader's acquaintance—was a middle aged man, who stayed with the Petersons only a couple of weeks, waiting the departure of a brig in which he was going to take passage for a port in South America. The man said very little about himself, except that he was bound abroad with the intention of bettering his fortunes, and had no particular idea of soon returning.

Once when I was there playing with Tom Peterson, a boy of my own age, this man, hearing him call my name in full, came down on the back stoop; and I remember his standing so long and looking so gravely at me that I noticed it, and felt a childish feeling of annoyance.

The next morning, he came around to Ephraim's, asked for me, drew me to his side, and looking at me again as before, inquired of Ephraim how I came to be there. Ephraim told him the history of the morning two years previous, and added what he had learned from me of my former life.

The man said he knew more concerning me than would do any good to tell; and that the name I went by was the right one. There were two big tears under his eyes, as he kissed me on the cheek. He thanked God over and over again that I had fallen in such good protection. He lifted his hands over me and fervently invoked a blessing on me—he was a devout man, as Mrs. Peterson informed Violet afterward—and, telling Ephraim that he might hear from him again at some future time, if he ever returned from abroad, our strange visitor departed.

But the trouble of names or an inquiry into my parentage, formed about the slightest of mine or Ephraim's cares. The vagabond child had not been left for twenty years uncared for, except by strangers, and unasked for, to make it likely that there would suddenly arise some mighty important story, to throw a romance about him and his affairs. I was not such a fool as to suppose so.

When I thought about it at all, which was very seldom, my mind had no other point to arrive at than the plain and evident supposition that my pedigree, if traced at all, as it appeared likely would never be the case, would be found in the lowest grade of society; and that my parents were doubtless dead long before this time.

Faith! it seemed just now as if there were a combination to agitate this subject, and hardly anything else. For in addition to poor crazy old Wigglesworth's mutterings, Lawyer Covert sent for Ephraim, and, under pretence of being interested in me, made minute inquiries concerning all the facts with which the reader is already acquainted. He even made Ephraim sit down, and repeat them to him deliberately; the morning when I came for my breakfast—the history of the cross-barred ring—and the incident of the stranger and his visit.

Probably it was, that Mr. Covert, in the activity of his heart, amused himself with making a fanciful story for me, when he had nothing else to do; often afterward, when I looked up from the desk, wearied and inwardly cursing the whole science of Law, with all its appurtenances and hereditaments, I would behold Mr. Covert gazing fixedly at me in what appeared to me a curious manner.

At the time I paid no attention to these things, nor to several other incidents that happened, and peculiarities in his treatment toward me. It was only after other developments were made that I recalled them. Of these, we shall have a true account in the course of the story.

CHAPTER XII.

The father, a character drawn from life. A revival meeting. An engagement with Wigglesworth.

THE WORLD HAS been favored with many portraits of religious fanatics—Methodists, Presbyterians, Roman Catholics, &c.; they are depicted in plays, in novels, and in poems. But they are generally wrong in one point; they do not make the enthusiast sincere. While in reality the religious enthusiast is always sincere. Moreover he or she is like all human specimens, a compound of both good and evil. As far as the enthusiasm of religion goes, it is not necessarily bad, but rather the reverse. Only it cannot altogether change other main portions of the character of the individual; they remain and give their stamp as before.

Calvin Peterson was not an exception to the above general rule. Nature made him with strong mental features. He had great resolution and fortitude; he could have borne, with savage endurance, any pains or penalties that came in consequence of his religious faith. It was indeed, rather a welcome thing to him to endure the little privations that resulted from that faith; and little annoyances are harder than great ones. But Calvin had none of the softer sentiments; or if he had, they were, in him, made hard and heavy in appearance. His affection for his family regarded their immortal welfare more than their temporal good; and the latter sometimes felt the effects of this partiality.

But it would be unjust to this man to deny that his strongest desire tended to what he considered the greatest and most enduring benefit of those whom he most cared for. It was simply his view of the case. In respect to the simple virtues of honesty and integrity Calvin was like a guileless child.

His son Tom, my friend, loved his father at heart; but it was a love which had not been cultivated and strengthened by mutual intimacy and good offices. It is often so with father and son. Tom thought his father too rigid, and the parent thought the young man too loose and irregular. Sometimes they had very serious disputes; and Tom, once in a while, almost thought he felt a repugnance to his own father.

While I was quite a boy, and Tom too, we would often go to the Methodist meetings.—Calvin Peterson was one of the shining lights here; and I have seen some pretty impressive spectacles under his exhortations. That there was a good deal of real devotional feeling, there could be no doubt.

A New York revival meeting! How strongly the impression remains upon me of one of these!

It was an agreeable autumn night, neither hot nor chilly. The windows of the church were partially open; for it was crowded inside. Crowded! why every seat and standing place, step and corner, were filled, crammed close and full.

You enter at the door, scanned sharply by a man who held the knob inside; you had felt his pressure as you opened the door, for he admitted no one quickly and gave you a solemn and satisfied stare, from head to foot. Perhaps he would, by signs, direct you to some part nearer the altar where you could find a seat by crowding closely.

"Come down, O, Lord! O, come down this night! Come right down here, O, Lord!"

With hands thrown in the air, and head turned upward, I saw Calvin Peterson, his face all wet with perspiration; and it was his voice I heard.

"Now brethren let us pray."

And Calvin's too was the voice of prayer. It was a violent, declamatory, passionate appeal to the Creator, who was spoken to in an earnest but familiar style, and invoked many times to come there, and be present in the midst of his worshippers. Nor was Calvin's prayer without feeling. He supplicated for all, for his own children, (Tom was with me, but had not the grace to feel the least affected,) for all the wicked, the poor, and the ignorant. Most of all, however, he wished an indescribable something, which appeared to be the most important requisite in making men what they should be.

"Touch our hearts with fire, O, Lord; break the rebellious rock; make us to see how wicked and utterly vile and helpless we are without Thee. O, send down thy spirit to be here, and dwell in the midst of us. Thy spirit is what we most need, and having that, we have all." &c. &c.

Toward the last of his prayer, Calvin struggled violently; for he had got the steam up, and was under full headway. The other men inside of the altar, and around it, they too swayed their bodies like trees in the wind. And many an Amen and emphatic groan were interspersed from these, during Calvin's prayer. And even if it all were without the formality and literary refinement of some other devotional outpourings—as it came thus fresh and genuine from the heart, why can we not suppose that it was as effective in the estimation of the Deity as even the most polished and elegant supplications?

The altar was fronted by a railing in the shape of a crescent; and this railing had at its foot a wide cushioned step, stretching the whole distance.

Kneeling on this step, as close together as they could be, were many young girls, and women, their faces bent in their hands, and some of them sobbing violently. Occasionally one of the men inside the railing would bend down and whisper to the girls, who however, appeared to make no answer.

"Pray for them, brothers, O, pray for them!" said Calvin, pointing to these girls, and to a number of men and boys, also, who were kneeling and crouching; some of them flat on the floor, all around the space near the altar.

And Calvin would occasionally come out and walk around among them, and, here and there stoop down and speak to them.

It was a good deal a matter of impulse with Mr. Peterson. Once, for example, at the close of a hymn, he spoke out in a loud voice:

"Let all those who love the Lord, rise from their seats."

There was a pause, and, sad to relate, only one individual, a pale, shamefaced young man, a tailor's apprentice, responded to the appeal.

Then they sang. This was the best part of it. For they sang with a will; and loved best the wild, almost grotesque tunes that there are so many of in America. What a strange charm there is in the human voice—so far ahead of instruments, to produce certain effects!

I could have listened to their singing all night. There was one song, in particular, intended to describe a contest between the soul's inclination to religion on the one side and worldly pleasure on the other.

"O, come my soul, and let us take,
An evening walk becoming thee,
But whither dost thou choose, we shall take our course,
O, to Calvary or Gethsemane

"But Calvary is a mountain high,
'Tis too difficult a task for me,
And I have heard there are lions in the way,
And they lurk on the path to Gethsemane."

Such were the two opening verses of this popular old camp-meeting song, which then went on to describe, in a manner worthy of John Bunyan, the struggle in the heart between the loves and lusts of the flesh as opposed to the dictates of duty. These strong, even vulgar, allegories always seize hold of the general feelings; and as for me, I love them yet.

In the singing, all joined who were so disposed; and, though to what is called a cultivated ear, there would probably be discord enough, the congregation present at meetings of this sort, have nothing of that to annoy them. Nor am I sure but what a truly cultivated musical taste would have experienced an unwonted charm in those fresh, quaint tunes and hymns.

At an advanced hour of the night, when all parties were pretty well exhausted, such a revival meeting as I have above described, broke up, and the congregation poured forth on their way homeward.

The revival meeting I have described, was as I remember them when Tom Peterson and myself, boys of fifteen and sixteen years, used to go of a Sunday evening, and sometimes during the week, to these assemblages. They are pretty much the same to this day.

Since we were grown up, however, both Tom and I were more delicate about going; for Tom had a very natural idea that his father did not make any great accessions to his dignity by his conduct at these revivals.

It was on his return from such a meeting—I having

been out pretty late myself, in a different scene—that I met Wigglesworth. The old man was in a high state of excitement. I attributed it to the religious fever which had now altogether penetrated him.

"Jack," said he, taking my hand, and speaking in a very earnest, hurried manner, "I want to have a serious talk with you."

"My dear old fellow," I answered, "it will all prove useless. I fear I shall prove a sinner for some years yet."

"No, no," he cried, in a still more impassioned manner, "it is nothing of that sort. It is about sin, to be sure, for it is about Covert. O, Jack! I shall unravel the most rascally tricks of that man to you—the most—"

"But, Wigglesworth, I am not Covert's keeper. These things do not concern me."

"Ah! there you are wrong again," cried the old man; "they do deeply concern you; they concern an innocent and much wronged orphan, whom that scoundrel has in his house, in a position little better than a servant. They concern your birth and fortunes. O! they concern many things."

"Old man," I said, a little excited now myself, "you are certainly out of your wits."

"I do not blame you for thinking so," he answered, "for I confess it is wondrous strange. But only hear me. Promise to come to my boarding house, and have a talk with me—let me see—the night after tomorrow, and you will change your mind."

To pacify him and start him homeward, as much as with any hope of learning what would interest me, I gave the required promise. Wigglesworth made me repeat it, and then went his way without another word.

CHAPTER XIII.

The Son, another character from life.—In company with a friend I visit Madame Seligny's.

TOM PETERSON WAS about the cleverest, finest, manliest fellow I ever knew; and I think as true a friend, at heart, as young men often meet with. Tom had all the best qualities of the hero of my childish admiration, mentioned aforetime as Billjiggs; added to which he possessed the cultivation which results from going to school, mixing a good deal with fellows, seeing life as it is to be seen in a great city like New York, and, most of all, from a warm generous heart, and a disposition to the enjoyment of life. His temper was happy and cheerful; his laugh, when he opened his mouth, and showed those great white teeth, was real music, that you couldn't get from fiddles or pianos. And when he laughed heartily, it was impossible not to think of the sunshine, or something of that sort.

Tom was a handsome dog withal, and used to take the feather out of my cap a little too often for my equanimity, in our acquaintance among the girls. But then he was always so good-natured about it, and not a bit vain or greedy, that one couldn't remain angry long. All my boyish confidences, and troubles and revenges and speculations, were known to Tom Peterson—I wonder that I haven't introduced him in this writing before. He saved my life once, when I was learning to swim. I had jumped overboard, like a fool, on the assurance of some Johnny Raw that once in deep water I would be certain to swim to the shore, when I found there was no other way of reaching it. Without Tom's efficient services then, there would never have appeared this entertaining history. We never had a fight or a quarrel together, which is a pretty strange thing for boys. It was more to my friend's credit than mine, too; when I showed anything like irritation or bad temper he would take refuge in silence, and in his own amiability. And he was amiable, without being the least bit of a coward; his tendency to peace and good will was part of a nature that could be brave as a lion when the occasion demanded.

The Lord love you, Tom Peterson, wherever you are this day! As far as I remember, you hated nothing which He has made.

What a blockhead old Peterson was to whine and mourn out his complaints over the sinful nature of this son! If a man couldn't be proud of such a son as Tom Peterson, he must be hard to please. Tom sinful! why he hadn't a drop of bad blood in his great broad-shouldered body!

But so thought not Calvin, the father. Especially was he horrified at Tom's intimacy with a lady, whose name he didn't know, but whose nature he felt sure, so the really grieved and unhappy old man told me, was next worst to the Prince of Darkness himself. For the alarmed father sought me out, knowing my friendship with Tom, and supposing I had influence over him; he sought me out and told me that the young man was sometimes absent from home all night, and, as near as could be found out, he spent his time in a splendid and seductive gambling house, kept by an old Jewess and her daughter, in great style, up town.

I really felt sorry for Peterson, although I could not promise to interfere, any further than to give Tom a chance to explain the matter, if he thought fit. At the same time, I comforted the grieved man, by reminding him how unlikely the story seemed. Tom was no saint, we all knew; but he had been equally free from any thing like dissipation, or coarse tastes.

"Have you spoken to him about these things?" I asked Calvin.

"No, not a word; I had not the heart to."

It seemed to me that this was a great pity; but I knew, from what Tom himself had told me, that the father and son took such different views of things; and I forbore to advise any further.

That very evening I made it my business to see Tom; and we took a walk together out into a park that lay at no great distance.

I opened the subject with some misgivings, and told the young man of his father's sorrow. He answered me with his natural frankness; and, as I suspected, the rumor which had come to the ears of the elder Peterson proved to be much ado about nothing. At the same time, the young man almost cried when I told him of his father's genuine distress.

"Come with me for half an hour," said Tom, "and then I will tell you all about it."

We walked up one of the Avenues for nearly a mile, and then turning round a corner, Tom stopped at a plain but elegant house, rang the bell, and was admitted.

"Tom Peterson and a friend," said he to the inquiring look of the servant who after drawing chairs for us in an open space at the side of the hall seemed to be waiting for something. The servant vanished instanter, and in a minute or two made his appearance again, and said—

"The ladies wish you to step up stairs."

We walked up and were shown into a richly furnished parlor, well carpeted, and with sofas, lounges and gas lights; the walls ornamented with pictures, and the corners with two or three voluptuous pieces of statuary.

One upon a sofa, and one upon a lounge, who should bless my sight than Mrs. Seligny and her showy looking black-eyed daughter Rebecca!

"We will sit down a moment," answered Tom to their polite invitation, "but only for a moment; as we cannot stay."

"That's a pity," said Rebecca, with an unmistakably loving glance at Tom, "for we are to have nobody here to-night; at least nobody we care for, if you go away."

"No doubt we are precious treasures," said Tom, laughingly, "but we can't stay more than fifteen minutes by the watch."

Mrs. Seligny spoke of Covert, whom she praised, though I thought it was with a dash of sarcasm. Rebecca bluntly expressed her opinion—interrupting her mother to that effect—that he was one of the greatest scoundrels in Wall street, or its neighborhood; apparently considering that she had put the case about as strongly as the English language allowed.

"Don't abuse him," joined in Tom, "for my friend here will fight in behalf of his very shoe-strings."

I disclaimed any intention of committing myself so deeply; and Tom added:

"Rebecca behaves like a true woman. She set her cap for the old man, and he is too cunning for her."

We all laughed at this sally, the young Jewess as much as the rest.

"You are mistaken there again," said she, "you put the saddle on the wrong horse."

"Tell the truth now; don't you go down to Wall street at least once a week, and try to captivate that innocent old man? And have you not lured him even into this house? Heaven only knows what you have done to him here!"

Rebecca laughed heartily.

"What would you say," cried she, "if you knew that not one hour ago this worthy gentleman was in the very room where we are now——"

"Aha! didn't I say so?"

"In this very room, making love to me!—making love, I tell you."

"And you accepted him?"

"Come, Tom, you are too bad."

"Well, tell me your answer to Covert, if this be true, and I have done."

Rebecca smiled mischievously.

"To confess the truth," said she, "I did not answer at all by word of mouth. I gave him a look, kicked over a footstool, and sailed out of the room with a magnificent bang of the door behind me——so."

And she rose, struck an attitude, frowned, gave Tom a good kick on the shins, and marched off with a comico-serious air, as of a tragedy queen, giving the same effect with the door wherewith she had celebrated her departure from the lawyer.

When Tom and I left this place and walked homeward—for that was the last we saw of the young Jewess that night—he told me all about it. My friend hadn't lived twenty-one years in the city, and grown up with the use of a pair of active legs and two tolerably sharp eyes, to be a perfect Joseph, nor to remain in the snowy preservation of pastoral simplicity. Favorite as he was with all who knew him, he had seen nearly every phase of town life, and had been, though not as a habituant, in all sorts of places.

Mrs. Seligny's was truly nothing more or less than a fashionable gambling house. Tom told me that if I had stayed till midnight, I could have found, on going down stairs, a magnificent suite of rooms, superbly furnished and lit up, and accommodated with the means for every sort of genteel gaming. Here visited many people, of many sorts; but over all, as if by silent consent, was thrown the thin veil of Mrs., or, as she was more often called, Madame Seligny's respectability, and decorous housekeeping. There was nothing worse than gaming, and even that not so deeply and unfairly as in many places of the sort.

Madame was fond of passing herself as the widow of an emigrant member of the French nobility; but she was neither more nor less than an old Jew tradeswoman. Rebecca was by no means the least attraction to the house; although, beyond presiding at the suppers, which she invariably did, she had very little to say to the visitors.

It was upon one of Tom's casual visits here with a friend that the young Jewess was interested in his welfare. She found means to inform him of her feelings; and after such a communication it was not exactly the nature of young Mr. Peterson to pack up his valise and leave in the first boat.

Of any thing in the nature of gambling, Tom was perfectly innocent. One reason was, he had no money; and another was, that he hadn't learnt without advantage the lessons of the practical student whose books are the things and men here in this great metropolis. Tom had cut his eye-teeth, although he couldn't join with his father Calvin in devotional performances.

The many nights that Mr. Peterson complained about

Tom's spending away, dwindled down to two; and Tom assured me that he had not neglected his business, nor drank a glass of liquor, the past three months.—And moreover there was not a straw beyond what he now told me.

"As to Rebecca," he wound up, "while I cannot feel indifferent to her, still you need not think I am in love. At least not yet.—The woman I love must be——; but never mind what. The night is late, and the best move we can make is for each to get himself to his virtuous bed."

CHAPTER XIV.

Retrospective. What I learn on another visit to Covert's house. I return to the office, and get a letter.

HOW THE TIME rolled on! The summer was nearly over, when the engagement was made to go and see Wigglesworth, as mentioned in Chapter Thirteen, and I had been the better part of two years with Covert. I had passed Cape Twenty-one, in the mean time, and was now legally a man. Violet, the good soul, celebrated the event by a grand supper, to which came Tom Peterson, and seven or eight of my more intimate cronies; and you may be sure that I did not forget Wigglesworth, although the latter was quite infirm, nor the progressive Nathaniel, nor Jack either. Wigglesworth, poor fellow, insisted upon repenting for his sins; but still he had been at the supper and was persuaded into having a good time.

I saw less of Inez than formerly, for she had taken up her permanent abode in half of Mrs. Fox's Cottage at Hoboken, where she amused herself with a garden and Nancy's children, of whom she was fond. Still I found time to make her an occasional visit. And whenever I went of a Sunday afternoon, which was my most frequent period of leisure, I was sure to bring home, for Violet, a huge bouquet; the source of which I made a great mystery of. And hence it came that Ephraim let off many jokes, at which nobody laughed more heartily than himself.

My good parents, all this while, had jogged on happily together, neither poor nor rich; although Ephraim had found it necessary to increase and enlarge his business, and the old milk depot was now transformed into quite an extensive provision or grocery store, doing a good business and bringing to us all a very fair income. Violet continued to help her husband about the store; for she would have it so, and could never, she said, be contented unless she had something stirring and lively to employ her mind and body about.

The excellent couple; how really, and how simply, they enjoyed life. With all their industry they had a wise way of never getting excited, nor overworking themselves, nor crying over spilt milk—or as Ephraim professionally used to say, sour milk.

As for me, what little I had picked up of law, was not of much account. The lapse of time had never reconciled me to the profession; although incidents and acquaintance and excitement, such as we in New York can easily meet with, diverted my attention from the despondency that had began to come upon me when I had been a student for the first few weeks. Inez too, had a share in rousing my gayety, and the vivacity that always resides in young veins.

My feelings toward the Spaniard could not be called by any means a profound love; at least so it seemed to me. For the only test I could imagine, gave that supposition a denial—I imagined how I should feel if Inez were to leave the city and never return; and, much as I liked the girl, I felt that her departure wouldn't break my heart. So I have picked up some threads of my story that had fallen away; and find myself at the morning of the day, where I was to go that night, and see Wigglesworth. I had made an engagement to that effect, it will be remembered, two evenings before.

This day was quite a day in my fortunes. First of all a discovery. Could I mistake those affectionate eyes, and the nimble fingers that had tied the handkerchief around poor Billjiggs' broken head? There, too, was the very same placid expression, and the goodness of heart, and the willingness to oblige.

Covert had been kept home by illness, and Wigglesworth being also absent, an unusual thing for him, I was under the necessity of going up to the lawyer's house several times. One of these times, in the room where I had to wait a while, there was an old portrait of a lady that seemed to me like one I had seen in a dream. It was a Quakeress, with the neat cap and neckerchief, painted with the manner of looking at you, which gives such vividness to a really good portrait. A long long time this picture riveted my attention; and then the truth came upon me like a flash of light!

That elderly lady—was it any one in the world but the hospitable nurse and helper of myself and my poor wounded friend, in the early times of vagabondism? There could be no mistaking it.

And now like another flash, came upon my mind, the looks of the young woman, who had opened the door for me, the night of the electioneering meeting; and whose face was then such a puzzle to me. She was the little girl of years before, remembered so well for a long time; indeed never forgotten; the little girl of the basement and the handkerchief.

If there were really anything in those hints of Wigglesworth, this, too must be the orphan to whom he alluded. The whole affair assumed an interest; and I determined to seize the first chance of making the acquaintance of the young Quakeress. I already knew that her name was Martha.

Fortune favored me; for Martha came into the room with her sewing basket, and telling me that Mr. Covert wished me to wait till he finished writing some papers which I was to take back to the office, she sat down, with one of those commonplace remarks about the weather, which are so often made in default of other conversational material.

"Whose portrait is that?" I asked.

"That is a lady thee has never seen," said Martha, "it is the portrait of Mrs. Covert, who died three years ago. I have reason to remember it. She was a second mother to me; and with her I passed, as a child, many happy years."

"You are mistaken about my never having seen her. And it is a good likeness."

The young woman looked up astonished; and without more ado, I gave a rapid sketch of the scene in the basement, and asked her if she did not remember it. Yes, she remembered it quite well.

"And was it thy wounded head I bound?"

"No; I was the other little loafer."

"Ah, yes; I remember, there were two boys; Mrs. Covert and I often spoke of thee and thy friend afterward."

Martha's countenance grew animated, and we talked of the good lady awhile. She had been the owner of some little property, and that, advanced in life as she was, must have been her fascination to Covert.

As Martha talked, the glow of feeling lit up her features, and she looked really beautiful. At the same time, there were traces of melancholy and lassitude about her, which I felt sorry to see. She avoided any reference to her father, except to tell me that her earliest childhood was passed with Mrs. Covert, both parents having died while she was but a year or two old; and of the latter she appeared to wish no inquiries about them. I saw that there was something connected with their history which made her withdraw from making any talk on the subject; for Martha's face to a very remarkable degree, was an almost provoking index to her heart and nature.

It seemed, after all, strangers that we were until this moment, that we were not strangers either, in fact; but old acquaintances. We fell at once into the friendly talk of persons who had that relation to each other.

Martha told me that Covert was her guardian; that after her parents' death she was taken altogether to his house, where she had lived agreeably with the old lady, the only absence being that she spent four years at a girls' boarding school. She spoke feelingly of Mrs. Covert's death, which had been a great trial to her.

That she was not happy here now, whatever might have been the case, I was convinced, from her demeanor and mode of answering my half-interrogation that way. For I had got so interested that I almost asked her.

The door opened, and there, looking yellower than ever, stood Mr. Covert in his dressing gown. He paused a moment, his eyes bent hard at us; and when he spoke there was more agitation, perhaps anger, in his tones than was usual for him:

"What have thee two to do or say together?"

Astonished at such abruptness, Martha dropped her work and looked at him in surprise. For my part, it was only because the man was so unmistakably ill that I refrained from giving him a very summary reply.

"Go Martha," he said, "and, young man, I tell thee, there is good reason why thee should not be so friendly here."

Martha rose hurriedly and, as she went out, I saw the unsuppressed tears falling rapidly from her eyes.

"You are pleased to talk in a manner I cannot understand, sir," said I, angrily.

"Doubtless, doubtless," he answered, sitting down, for he seemed to grow faint, "but thee can at least understand that I do not wish any intimacy between Martha and thee."

His eyes were bright with passion. Was it for me to bandy words with this sick man—and upon something it seemed as though we neither of us knew what we were talking about?

I took the papers I had been waiting for, and left the house.

I stopped by the way for an hour or more, to see Tom Peterson. Tom was by trade a machinist, and, young as he was, had arrived at the station of foreman in a large thrifty establishment, whose proprietors thought a good deal of him, and trusted him more than any one else in their employ. Was it not that this manly trade had something to do in forming my friend's character? I had a notion that way, and a vague feeling of the story it was that had caused a good deal of my repugnance to the law.

Tom had gone to his trade eight years before, from his own choice; and he was now considered as thorough a workman as any in the land. He got good wages, and, as it was well understood that such a man as he could not be picked up everywhere, my friend was very independent, and demanded of the wealthy gentlemen who hired him, the same civility toward himself which he invariably used toward them.

You see I like to talk about Tom Peterson. And, reader, it would have done you good had you known him. He was such a fine specimen of a young American mechanic.

I told my friend of my visit to Covert's house, and of Martha, and the lawyer's indignation.

"He's a bad man," rejoined Tom, bluntly, "and I tell you what, Jack, although it's none of my business, if I was you, I'd cut loose from him and his affairs as soon as possible. Rebecca Seligny is the sharpest woman to understand a fellow's character that I ever saw; and she despises him. Why the fellow, as sanctified as he looks, is carnal enough, according to her story. She is mad at the sound of his name."

"She likes you better," said I, waggishly.

"Could she show a better sign of taste and judgment?" responded Tom. "But don't let us say anything more about Rebecca. I expect we shall quarrel soon; for the dear girl is very exacting."

Tom's advice was not so much different from my own feelings, as to make me think no further about it. And I had now begun to feel enough interested in Martha, to want to know something more.

Nathaniel and his dog stopped from their exercise—they had been commemorating the absence of all hands from business by running races up and down the walk in front—they stopped and came up stairs with me when I reached the office.

"You return in good time, Don Cæsar," said Nat, "for a messenger from the Princess has just left this for you."

He gave me a note. I thought the boy was fooling, and tossed it back to him. But he grew serious, and told me that it was brought but a moment before by a little darkey, who, in answer to Nat's inquisitiveness, could only say that it was given to him by a young lady, with a shilling to bring it down as addressed.

I opened it, and read as follows:

"I write this immediately on your departure.

"This is no time to stand on ceremony; and I will follow the impulse of my heart. Alas! I have so few friends that it will not do for me to lose the chance of one, although I may seem immodest in writing so. Few? Where, indeed, have I any?

"I am unhappy here, to a degree which I will not undertake to narrate upon paper. I was much interested in your description of your adopted parents, Ephraim Foster and the good Violet. I wish to know them. I wish to speak with them.

"I have not time to continue my discordant note; but come at once to the point. Will you—for I must ask it—will you, unless you hear from me again, call for me tomorrow evening, and show me to Foster's house, and introduce me to him and his wife?

"You will then learn the reason of my singular request. —M."

At dinner time, I showed this note to Violet and prepared her for the visit. Her motherly heart always warmed toward those who had fallen in distress; and it was plain that poor Martha was suffering under troubles of no ordinary character.

CHAPTER XV.

A strange history revealed.—
Mr. Covert's conduct accounted for.

I COULD ONLY sit and listen, without saying a word, then; for such a web of villainy and romance quite took away my breath! Was my mind under the influence of no dream? Had I not been overpowered with some work of fiction? No. I looked deliberately about the little attic bedroom; and there was the high window, and on another side Wigglesworth's lank bed, with its check coverlid; and near by the antiquated washstand, and the table by which we sat, and on which lay a package of manuscript; and, leaning against the wall an odd chair, and all lit up by the lamp giving its flickering light.

And there in the kind of seat called a Boston rocker, sat poor old Wigglesworth himself. Although he had been out that afternoon, towards dark, and had a long interview with Martha, it was more than he ought to have done. I was quite shocked with the ghastly appearance of the poor old man, and his lurid and bloodshot eyes! He could not be long for this world. Indeed he told me he didn't think he should have lived till the present hour, except that he thought he had one work to perform. And he couldn't rest in peace, if it was not done.

"I tell you Jack," said he, excitedly, "this is all that has kept me up for a long while past. As for my body, it gave out months ago. It is dead I tell you; you can see that for yourself."

Poor creature! you did look more like a corpse, that moment, than a living being.

"The mind, Jack," the old man went on, "I never before thought it had such wonderful power. But I *resolved* to live until I had unravelled the web of deviltry which, as I have told you, I providentially got the clue of; I *determined* that I would last till this revelation could be made—was made. And now, O my God, I thank thee!"

He motioned to me to hand him a glass of water from the stand. When he had taken it, he continued:

"You will know without my telling you that I soon after my engagement in his office found out Covert to be a villain. I knew, too, that he had, as Martha's guardian, control over quite an extensive property; but, bad as he was at heart, I did not until lately believe him so utterly vile as not only to defraud her of her inheritance, but to make that friendless girl a victim to his licentious passions."

I started. And now, ah! I began to see the meaning of

Martha's note, and its hidden allusions. Wigglesworth went on:

"Martha's affairs involve a peculiar history, extending many years back. The package on the table there was written by her father—written in prison, where he was confined for a terrible crime done in the heat of passion. That crime, with his imprisonment, and his death, could not but exercise a gloomy effect upon her; although she was an infant when they occurred.

"Poor girl! the more I have learned the more I am interested about her; and this afternoon's interview with her decided me to unburthen the whole matter, without any reserve, to you. It was for the better understanding of it all, that Martha gave me her father's story, prepared by himself, which reached her from a trusty source, sometime since, and which she has kept, unknown to Covert. Take this packet, then Jack; but do not read it till you have leisure to weigh well what you read. Some evening let it be, when you are alone, for there is weighty stuff in it. And though you already know the particulars which are contained in it, you have perhaps a right to hear the witness of him who made you fatherless, and to know how deeply he repented and suffered for it."

Truly it was more like romance than sober life, in a dwelling in one of the streets of this matter-of-fact-city. And, after I had buttoned the manuscript in my breast-pocket, I had to thump there from time to time to convince myself that I was really awake.

As I rose to bid him good night, Wigglesworth took my hand between his, and I felt those feeble palms, thin and cold!

"Jack," said he, "do not think I wander in my thoughts; but I know that I have not many days, perhaps many hours, more to live. I have left some few directions with the landlord who keeps this place. He is an honest man whom I have known for years and I am sure he will obey them faithfully. You will think me something of an aristocrat, Jack, but I wish to be buried in my mother's vault—she was of the old English stock, the early ones here, Jack—in Trinity churchyard. That will cost money, too, as the city regulations are now; but I have long provided for that, and my landlord, who knows my wish, is my banker. You shall go with my old friend—probably, indeed, none but you two—and see that my shattered hulk is put away there, according to my wish. Will you not Jack?"

I strove, although it went somewhat against the grain, for I felt a profound sadness; I strove to answer in a cheerful manner, and told him that we might have many a pleasant supper together yet, and that he would get over his illness and come out a new man.

The old clerk made no response, for he saw that my cheerfulness was labored. That chilling, feeble pressure of his thin, pulseless hands, at parting: it sends a palsy through me, as I remember it now.

Only when I got out in the cool open air, and slowly, very slowly, took my way home, did the information I had gathered that evening take consistent form and shape, and spread out before me in a manner that I could realize, and bring it home to myself as a tangible history.

To myself! Yes, it concerned me, as nearly as the young Quakeress, of whom Covert was the guardian. Strange that our interests were, after all, so closely connected together. And not only our interests but our very lives—bound by a doubly-solemn tie.

Yes, myself! From what Wigglesworth had gathered, I at last knew of myself. The old man had been indefatigable; and truly, as he said, for the last few months, had lived but for hardly any other purpose than to investigate and make plain the mystery. He had even, by dint of the closest inquiry, going backward many years, sought out the whereabouts and particulars of the strange visitors, who, years before, boarded with Calvin Peterson, and whose visit to Ephraim's and real or apparent knowledge of me and my origin, I have mentioned in a former chapter. This man, Wigglesworth pursued the track of: he discovered the place to which he sailed; and that he had settled there, and was living there yet. The old clerk entered into correspondence with him, and his information corroborated what he had before suspected.

In many other ways—in every way—by examining the records of courts—by retrospective searches in every quarter—the ardent old man had come to such a state of certainty as to leave no room for doubt or disbelief. Moreover, accompanying the manuscript which he gave me, were papers that fortified to a point of positive proof, every point of the following strange narrative.

Martha's father was a young man of what the followers of Penn call the World's People; it was only her mother who belonged to the Quaker sect. The match, however, was one altogether for love. They had no other child but the little girl. They were possessed of very considerable wealth, and lived in comfortable style, in a house he owned, just near enough to the great metropolis to give him all the advantages of its luxuries and its intellectual enjoyments, and just far enough away for him to possess the pleasures of country freedom and space. For the husband was a man of some literary taste, and, young as he was, he had seen much of the world, having travelled both abroad and in America.

Like the blast of death, or the trumpet of the destroying angel, there came, in the twinkling of an eye, something that destroyed at once all these blessings, present and in perspective!

A horrible occurrence, none the less deadly in its consequences because it was partly the result of one of those fearful and accidental liabilities to which any man, or family, might be subject, came to wither the happiness of a loving husband and wife; and have a future effect on a beautiful and innocent child! The husband and wife bent to the destructive blow, and lifted not their heads from the ground—in which they sought nothing better than quiet graves. The child was too young to feel the horror that overwhelmed her parents. She grew up under other fostering care, into the beautiful and tender-natured, but still bold and energetic, Martha.

This fearful thing was, that the husband, in a moment of excessive irritation, struck one of his workmen, who had somehow offended him, a deadly blow on the head. It caused death—and that death by a coincidence that made my blood chill—was none other than the death of my own father!

Again I had to connect in my mind, link by link, the inevitable chain of evidence that Wigglesworth had gathered, before I could believe anything so much like romance.

The murderer was arrested, put in confinement, and, in due time, arrived the day appointed for his trial.

But that day he never saw. He was in prison but a few hours, when his young wife, overwhelmed with these dismal misfortunes, died of a broken heart. And, after that, he sank, slowly but surely, into decay; and only asked to be buried by her side.

Yet during the days before his death, his mind, which seemed to have been of great natural resolution, did not fail him. He arranged his worldly affairs with great circumspection, drew up most of his own papers under legal advice, and had them properly certified and recorded. He made his will, in which he did not forget the offspring of the poor workman, his victim—It is useless to deny that I both look upon the slain man, and feel toward him, nothing more than as I would look upon the same gloomy fate, befalling a stranger. And is it wonderful that it is so? He was, indeed, though my parent, really a stranger. Our feelings are the creatures of association and education; and, even while my brain felt the shock, through sympathy, that must have followed all those events, I thought of them more as a listener to the story, than as one having any special point of interest that came home pointedly to me.

And, reader, that is the way I feel about it to this day. I will have the merit of candor, if I have not of sensitive feelings.

The day appointed for the trial, found the accused man before a higher tribunal than any here on earth. It was the day on which he was buried by the side of his wife; and then the affair, which had been much talked about, and will even now be remembered by some perhaps who read these lines, dropped away gradually from the public mind.

It so happened that the principal legal adviser for Martha's father, during the few weeks of his imprisonment, was Covert, then just commencing the practice of the profession. He so wrought upon the young man's mind, distracted with his condition, as to be appointed guardian of his infant daughter, and to get the general control of his estate. Although the father was prudent enough to put certain checks on Covert's movements, and effect, to some extent, a superior control over that cunning villain; the main object of which had been for many years, on the part of the lawyer, to circumvent and get out of the way.

Calvin Peterson's pious boarder, who had come to see me at Ephraim's, was my father's brother. One of his answers to Wigglesworth stated that my mother's death took place a year or two before my father was killed; and that I was their only child.

By the copies of documents which Wigglesworth put me in possession of, it appeared that the will of Martha's father directed the settlement of one third of his fortune upon the offspring of, as he termed it, his victim. This item, and the specific directions regarding it, appeared to have been prepared and recorded with all the forethought which characterized the arrangement of his other affairs.

Covert, undoubtedly, at some pains and care to himself, kept this point a secret. For he was made thoroughly aware of the wishes of that unfortunate gentleman, and of the fact that the slain workman had a little child, who would be turned loose upon the world uncared for.

That he wished the sole management of the property, intending it should eventually come into his own hands, was enough to make him lie low, in the beginning. It was also enough, afterwards, when he learned, as he did learn, that the little lost waif had turned up in the student of his own office to make him continue the game of deceit and falsefacedness.

Undoubtedly, after my father's death—for I was too little to remember any thing at all about it—I had been turned from door to door, in some way escaping the cold charities of the alms-house, as I was, it seems, not absolutely without the power of locomotion. But I have already treated to a sufficient degree on that part of my history; and, if there is any thing more wanting, the reader must supply it from his or her imagination.

CHAPTER XVI.

What was determined on in a family council.

THE NEXT DAY, which was Sunday, like a fellow who is burthened with more than he can carry, I took Tom Peterson into my confidence, and told him the whole of events and revelations of the night before. Tom opened his eyes, when he found out that I was really serious. I had already imparted all of them to Violet and Ephraim; who were confounded beyond measure and wished to reflect the whole day before concluding what course to take.

It was a pleasant Sunday forenoon, and Tom and I crossed the North River, to Hoboken, and strolled along to Inez' cottage. A sudden thought seized me, as I saw the happy and lovely appearance of that little dwelling, where the joint labors of Inez, Nancy, and four or five out of the eight little Foxes, had caused vines to bloom, and pleasant shrubbery, and some late flowers that were quite gay, even at this advanced season.—Nancy herself was out there in front, and welcomed me, and told me to go up at once in the second story, and make myself and my friend at home in Inez' sitting room.

Verily this was a day of telling news, and making confidants. For I again went over the whole history of Martha, to the dancing girl, and asked her whether, in case it was necessary, she would take the Quakeress under her protection and hospitality for a short time.

"That I will," said she, with spirit, "and if Mr. Covert dares set his foot here, against the young woman's will, Nancy and I will salute him with such a reception that he won't forget us, years to come."

I told Inez that I might require her to make her words good; and that if so, I would give her due warning. She told me not to be afraid of calling in her assistance; and that she only wanted a good chance to take a little revenge on Covert for his intentions toward her spare cash.

It seemed that it was somewhat as I suspected when Inez came down to the office, many months before. The shrewd Spaniard, from some cause or other, had her suspicions aroused, waited a few weeks before purchasing the stock which Covert recommended, and in which Ferris was interested, and then a few weeks longer; and then had the satisfaction to read in the papers how the whole edifice, stock and all of Mr. Pepperich Ferris's wonderful company had tumbled to the ground—and how luckily her dollars just escaped.

You may be sure, the mettlesome Spaniard had fire

enough in her veins to resent the deliberate design of cheating her, almost as much as if it had been successfully accomplished. For that it was a deliberate design, there could be no dispute.

Even Mr. J. Fitzmore Smytthe came in for his share of the high-strung girl's displeasure. And, at his next visit, Inez saluted him with such a voluble and fiery tongue, that this genteel and taciturn individual was fain to put his fingers in his ears and beat a retreat in double quick time. That he had received his walking papers, however, was a work of special grace to me; I by no means mourned his absence from Inez's rooms when I visited there; considering in such cases that two made a much pleasanter party than three.

When we returned to New York, I bespoke the services of Tom Peterson, too; for I had a scheme in my head. Tom promised to do anything for me, from tossing Covert out of his own window to holding the light while I wrote him a challenge.

When Martha, that night, under my charge, according to the request made in her note, left Covert's house—he was confined to his room yet, fortunately—I felt that it would perhaps be better for her to go back no more. She was now free from the wretch's premises, and why should she place herself in his power again?

I proposed this, in full family council; and it was considered favorably, until Martha herself put the negative on it. She said that it was her intention to leave, but not tonight.

She knew, too, that she would be under the necessity of leaving clandestinely; for Covert had all the restlessness and suspicion of a guilty mind. An additional reason was that there were sundry articles, and some important documents which she must take away with her when she did go.

For Covert had not all the cunning of the game on his side. Wigglesworth and the young Quakeress, during the three days past, had made some master-moves; and, deep as I knew the lawyer to be, it seemed, when I heard all, that they were likely to countermine him. Above all they had the advantage of working unknown to him. Little did the scamp suspect that, all the while he was tied there to his bed-side, the girl whom he looked upon as his helpless victim, and whom the disgusting brute intended as his victim in a double sense, was quietly, with the invaluable help of his clerk, who knew more about his affairs than any other person—was quietly, I say, digging the very ground from under his feet.

It had been the lawyer's policy, by slow degrees to get the property which was left by Martha's father, to be made use of as directed in his will; this property it was Covert's design, steadily pursued, year after year, to get transformed into paper representatives, such as government or state bonds, certificates of deposite, and so forth. Indeed, it was the persevering and mysterious course of this proceeding that aroused Wigglesworth's first suspicions; he knew that the property belonged to Martha, that it was first well and reliably invested; and that, in being sold, it was frequently sacrificed, and a loss suffered on the second purchase, without any gain. As to Martha, she was ignorant of business, and without knowing why or wherefore, signed almost every paper that Covert presented to her.

The best and most important move of all, was, that Wigglesworth had made use of his knowledge of Covert's affairs, to give Martha such instructions and such a description of the papers—her name was specified in every one of them where a name was necessary, and they were undeniably hers—that she had found out where the lawyer kept them in his house, and was prepared to pounce upon and take possession of them, when she got a good opportunity, and bear them off. A woman and a lawyer's clerk, have they not some sharpness?

All these things being discussed in the family council, it was determined that there was no time to be lost. Covert might discover the plans that were making headway against his vile machinations, and use his lawyer tricks in such a way as to stop us all off. We decided therefore that Martha should leave his house, for good, the next night. Violet and Ephraim would willingly have had her take up her abode with them; but it was thought best, instead, to accept the offer of Inez, which I mentioned, and whom I promised to notify the next day.—These points were conned over and decided in short metre; for Martha was to be home again at nine o'clock. When I waited upon her back, I told her I hoped she would not be discouraged, nor fail me, at the appointed time, which we purposely put at midnight for greater security. The stout-hearted girl assured me that if she were living it should be as we planned it out, unless our plans failed by means other than any that depended on her.

My sleep was disturbed that night by Martha's fortunes; and I half-dreamed of the homicide in which our two different parents had played so sad a part. I forgot to say that Martha herself had not yet learned of my being the son of her father's victim. I had charged Ephraim and Violet to be careful of mentioning this to her. Wigglesworth I knew would not.

Among the first things I attended to, next forenoon, were, the dispatching of a note to Inez by a trusty hand, and then calling on Tom Peterson, whose help I engaged in a way that we shall understand by and by.

I asked Nathaniel if I could have his assistance that evening carrying off a princess from a tormenting monster. The young gentleman informed me that whatever man dared, he would dare. I told him I was serious. As for him, he but loved too well any thing in the shape of an adventure, especially if it was to be on my responsibility.

I would have felt some qualms about stealing Martha away in this manner, if I hadn't been so sure that subtlety must be opposed to subtlety; and that, if Covert had anything like open and premature defiance he would in all likelihood outwit us all. But once safely away, Martha in possession of the afore-mentioned valuable papers and bonds, I felt that we could make a stout fight against him.

Besides, I had the array of documents, and an index of scores more to prove, if the event needed, the thoroughness and veracity of my narration. These Wigglesworth had given me, the evening of our memorable interview.

Poor old man! I stepped up a moment to see him. He lay on his narrow bed, without uttering a word, and looking wan, and wasted to a skeleton, but still with an expression of peace in his countenance. I bid him a mental farewell, for I doubted whether I should ever see him alive again.

CHAPTER XVII.

An escape attempted, and what happened during the same.

THE APPOINTED hour arrived, and there I was ready—ready, and away with my prize! Martha, I saw by the flashing of a lamp as we passed, looked as pale as ashes; but there could be no mistaking the resolution, amounting to sternness, in her eyes. Her compressed lips, too, and that whole expression of her features, were so unusual as to give her an appearance I had never remarked in her before. Could the gentle Quaker girl, indeed, have all this time, contained such elements of spirit and promptitude? I had not understood her properly, that was certain.

Nat hurried to us, from the corner near by, where he had been waiting. He had his dog Jack with him, and the two, with a certain activity, were more quiet than usual for them.

"Mr. Peterson and I've got the boat waiting," said Nat, "and we'll soon row you over."

As for that, if it were necessary, I could take a hand myself, thanks to the practice which most New York boys get along her docks and shores.

Nat told us that he had almost given us up, and was just on the point of departure. He supposed that some unforeseen obstacle intervened, and Martha's flight had been postponed to a more convenient season.

Martha's bundle; I gave it to Nat with a great caution of its importance.

We hurried rapidly along the streets, Martha holding to my arm, though she needed little support; for the brave girl felt in this emergency of her life, as she afterward told me, fully capable of tracking her own part, even should some still more eventful crisis occur, and should she become deprived of my support.

Nat, carrying the parcel which Martha had brought away, was the only cause I had for disturbance. Our quick steps, and a certain flutter which could not be avoided, in our demeanor, joined with this parcel, I feared, might arouse the inquisitive suspicions of the watchmen. I at first thought of directing Nat to keep some distance behind us; but as we didn't know exactly the locality of the dock where, as he informed us, the boat lay; and indeed, as we took our course from street to street, and hurried around corner after corner, without settled plan—there was no other way than to stick together and ruin our chances.

"What is your hurry, neighbors?" saluted our ears, as a watchman stepped out from the doorway of a corner grocery we were wending by.

I looked him as coolly as I could in the face, and asked him what he meant by stopping us in that manner.

"No offence," said he, "only I always try to do my duty."

"Well what has your duty to do with us?"

"Perhaps nothing, and then, again, perhaps something," was his answer.

I suppressed my annoyance as well as I could, when Martha, with woman's instinct, remarked, with a quiet tone:

"Now friend, do not prevent us; but take this shilling and refresh thyself with some coffee, and let us go on our way peaceably."

The gentle voice of Martha, whose manner showed her to be so different from what the guardian of the night no doubt supposed, reassured him probably more than the coin, and he said he did not mean any harm, but he had to look out and do his duty.

We hurried on as before, and were within a couple of squares of the river, when we were suddenly stopped, from behind, by two watchmen, one of whom laid a hand firmly on my shoulder.

"What's your hurry, this dark night?" he said coolly.

I didn't like his tone at all. If there be any thing in a man's voice to judge his intentions by, he was a different fellow from the one whose good offices we had escaped, a few minutes before. Besides, there were two of 'em; and, in such a case, a little gratuity was not likely to have any effect.

"What have you in that bundle?" said he to Nat.

I felt Martha's arm tremble a little, but she answered distinctly.

"The young man carries some clothing and other things, that belong to me."

"Are you sure they have always belonged to you?" said he.

"Perfectly sure," said Martha, with a self-possession that fully equalled that of her interrogator.

"And what is your name"? He asked again.

Martha made no answer to this question; and there was a pause, which I felt to be an awkward one.

"That can be of little consequence," said I, "and you must excuse her from answering your question."

"There's no harm, or disgrace, in honest men, or women either, telling their names," said he, peering sharply into Martha's face.

She stood his look without wincing, but still made no reply.

"Ladies do not care about such avowals, to all people, honest and delicate as they may be," said I, for want of something better to say, "but I will cheerfully give you my address."

He took the parcel from Nat, although that young gentleman showed signs of a somewhat pugnacious spirit, and refused at first to give it up, preferring as he said, to keep it in his own possession, until demanded by some authority having a proper right. But I signed to him to make no opposition as I supposed the officer wished to see if there were any special evidences wherefrom he might come at once to some judgment on the good or bad ground of his suspicions.

The bundle had been put up in haste, and so far went to justify an inference unfortunate to us. But it appeared to satisfy him that it contained no articles of weight; and he after balancing it a moment in his hands, the feeling of it, and turning it over, returned it to Nathaniel. The boy took it angrily and favored him with a scowl which would have been appropriate enough in deep tragedy. The watchman, however, paid not the smallest attention to the angry youngster.

"Remain a moment just as you are," said he; and stepped a couple of paces aside, and conferred with his companion.

We felt that it would not be safe to pursue any other course than the one which was forced upon us. Martha and I, in a subdued voice, argued the feasibility of bribing them, or attempting it; but there was more danger than chance of success in that; and we relinquished it. The one who had first spoken then stepped back, the silent gentleman appearing to leave everything to the direction of the other:

"You are probably very honest people," said he, "and as good as I am myself. But I think it best for you to go with me to the police quarters on the next block; you will not, I think, have to stay more than a few minutes. At least I hope so."

I commenced to remonstrate with him, but he was firm. There was nothing left us, but to follow his orders.

Even now, although the circumstances would seem to be enough to try the temper of a strong-minded man, I could see no signs of alarm or disturbance on Martha's part. She clung a little closer to me, but her look was as composed and her walk just as even and self-reliant, as before.

Master Nat, however did not by any means take it so philosophically. He declined going at all, and there seemed some chance of a disturbance; for the officers turned sternly to him, and one of them raised his arm. Jack growled and erected the hair of his neck. A moment more, and there would probably have been a fight; for when Nat's blood was up, and Jack's too, they would have made battle with St. George's dragon himself.

"What," said Martha, stepping to the boy, and, as she stood between him and the constable, laying her hand on his shoulder, "thee will not desert us now, when we want thy help the most."

It was enough. The premeditated tempest was quelled. Nat picked up the parcel from where it dropped on the flag-stones, tucked it under his arm, chirped for the dog to follow him, and without a word further trudged, with cast-down eyes, to meet the same fate as ours.

The distance to the police station was soon reached, and we entered the front way, passed through to the back room, and there waited the pleasure of our captors.

Two or three half-dozing men were on a wooden settee in the room. One of them rose and civilly brought a chair for Martha, who sat down. I stood with my hands on the back of the chair, not feeling very well at ease. Nathaniel rested himself on a stool near by, and Jack, evidently aware that there was now leisure for it, stretched himself at full length on the floor, and had a good time with his head between his fore-paws.

CHAPTER XVIII.

In which is told the end of the scrape—
and what came to pass afterwards.

NEW AS AN ADVENTURE and situation of this sort were to Martha, she stood it like a heroine. I had never seen a woman's conduct more admirable; and, from that moment, my attachment—for such a feeling had already taken root on my mind—was colored with an esteem and respect which made it indeed true love. Previously, the sentiment had perhaps been composed more of pity and sympathy for the wrongs which were encompassing her; but the demeanor she exhibited in these incidents, proved her worthy of a more solid regard, and warmer friendship.

Yes, it was while we were waiting there in that cheerless police room, that the inspiration first came to me, of a simple way to cut the knot at once; or, at any rate to remove most of the complications, and make the battle between Covert and Martha a decided one. I felt, I knew, that such a girl as this I could love. Indeed, I felt that I did love her, now; and that my feeling was of that positive, real kind, equally without reserve, and devoid of morbid ardor—a feeling which I divined was the best and the only genuine feeling which should lead to marriage.

I bethought me then—for though we waited but a few minutes, thought travels over space and time quick enough—and I bethought me of the little girl in the basement, years before. I saw the scene before me—the good protectress in her plain cap, and the smooth hair parted on her head. I thought of my early crony, Billjiggs. The good lady—ah! How gently she washed that dirty head, while I held the large basin of half-warm water; how the jagged wound made me almost feel sick, although one who helped bring Billjiggs in, pronounced it not so much after all, and laughed, and said that it was more blood than anything else. How the lady looked around, and, finding nothing else handy, took that famous handkerchief, so large, so fragrant, of such beautiful white linen, and bound up Billjiggs's phrenological developments from the public gaze. Then how the little girl Martha came and neatly tied the knot, with such tender fingers, for fear she might hurt the wound. Even then, did she not exhibit the inward force and strength of her character?—Wouldn't almost any other little girl have been frightened and held back in alarm?

And thus and so, under a semi-arrest, and not knowing but what we would have to pass the night in durance, was determined the love of Jack Engle.

In a few minutes, the man who had brought us hither,

came up to us and asked for the bundle. He wished to take it away.

"To that I must object," said Martha, turning to him, "and I do not know if thee has any right to do so."

Martha was a different person to deal with, from the boy Nat, and the officer felt it.

"Then let the boy bring the things," said he, "and all of you come in here."

We followed him into an adjoining room. At a little wooden table there was seated the captain of the district. The moment I saw him I felt relieved; for he was an old acquaintance of Ephraim Foster's, and, besides, he and I knew each other well. Although older than I, he was yet a young man, and we had spent many months in the same studies at the public school.

"What, Jack Engle," he cried, looking up; and then turning to the man who had brought us in, "Oh, Jones, your trouble is all for nothing. These people cannot possibly be anything to *that* affair."

"Well, if you know them," answered Jones, "that's enough, of course."

The officer, in a civil tone, but without showing any vexation or disappointment, asked our excuses, said that the captain would tell us why he had been so particular, and then left the room.

My school-friend good-naturedly rose, and pushing his seat along to Martha, informed me how there had been a good deal of serious pilfering in that neighborhood—that from information obtained by the officers, he supposed a still more daring robbery was on foot that very night—and that a female was concerned with the parties in it. Their information was not exact enough to point them specifically to the premises endangered nor to the thieves; but they were more than usually on the lookout. Under such circumstances, we happened to fall in the way of one of the most vigilant of the officers. The captain hoped we would have philosophy enough to overlook the annoyance.

Martha's now cheerful face assured him that there was no great harm done. Truly, that face alone was enough for a passport of honesty through all the police stations of the land. Steady young man as my friend, had reason (I hope,) to set me down for, from all he knew of my past life, one look at the aforesaid face was enough to reassure him against any suspicions from our situation. For although we were cleared of any darker imputation, there was something that might be supposed worth elucidating in being out at this hour of the night, or rather morning, scudding rapidly through the streets with a woman, a bundle, a boy, and a dog.

But the captain did not by word of mouth ask any explanation. And as I did not think the real circumstances fitting to a voluntary recital of the facts, I bid him good night, and we departed.

We soon reached the wharf, where Tom Peterson was on the alert for us. Nat's boat had not been disturbed; and I helped Martha down into it, and laid my overcoat over the seat for her to sit on. Jack entered with a bound after Nathaniel sprang in, and with a push from Tom off the pier, we were afloat.

Then I felt relieved indeed. It seemed to me that we were now free from Covert's more direct machinations, at all events. He might plot as much as he liked, but his presence and the sound of his voice could not trouble us more.

Martha, too, entered into these feelings. She had suffered much from her situation in Covert's house, after his wife's death; although her simplicity and vigor of mind had shielded her from things that would have been sore trials to ordinary girls. Within the past few weeks, in particular, she had found growing up in her mind a settled repugnance to the lawyer. Her sentiment towards him, during the lifetime of his wife, had been one more deserving to be called indifference than any thing else. She did not particularly dislike; but at the same time she had no attachment, and nothing more than a very ordinary respect for him. Since the developments of late, as was to be expected, she could no longer occupy a neutral position. Her character had a good deal of strong impulse in it; and this was directed in a manner anything but favorable toward her legal adviser and hitherto controller.

We rowed out in the river; I pulling on one side, Tom's oar on the other, and Nat acting as steersman. Jack was at the prow, with his nose elevated, and making quite a figurehead for our little craft. Martha looked upward at the sky, and evidently enjoyed the whole scene. Though there was no moon, the stars were shining bright. The fresh south breeze came pleasantly up from the Narrows; the water dashed in ripples against our boat; and altogether it was indeed a soothing and refreshing half-hour, after the hurry of Martha's escape, and the stoppage at the police house.

Out in the middle of the river, we lay on our oars a few minutes, and enjoyed the scene still more. The long stretch of the city's shores was silent and hushed; two or three sloops, at various distances on the river, moved along, their white sails showing like great river ghosts; and not a harsh sound was to be heard.

The Hoboken shore, too, was solitary and still. As we neared it, the just-risen moon shone out from a cloud, and scattered a flood of light on the wooded banks, the water, and every thing else. It seemed like a good omen, and, indeed, could hardly help having that effect on us all. The river, up above, which had seemed like a path of darkness and doubt, was now sparkling; the sails of the sloops looked like things of real life again; and the round heights of Weehawken had their sombre shadows touched up into varied gray and dark green. From a war-vessel lying off Castle Garden, came the sounds of bells striking the time, and the sonorous voice of the watch.

We stepped ashore, full of spirits and with the young blood in us aroused to the vigor of renewed life, and hope, and action. Tom and Nat tied the boat, and the latter took his bundle again, while the former remained until our return. Jack coursed to and fro like a mad creature.

A good walk brought us, not at all tired, to Inez' cottage. She was up and expecting us. She kissed Martha on the cheek and welcomed her warmly. Our troubles and adventures were over for that night, at any rate; for, though Tom and I had to row back home, and had a good time in so doing, we hardly spoke a word, and met with nothing worth mentioning. I had hardly got in bed when I heard the advance movements of Ephraim, who was an early riser.

CHAPTER XIX.

Some hours in an old New-York church-yard; where I am led to investigations and meditations.

IN THE EARLIEST chapter of my life, speaking of Wigglesworth, I alluded to the melancholy spectacle of old age, down at the heel, which we so often see in New York—the aged remnants of former respectability and vigor—the seedy clothes, the forlorn and half-starved aspect, the lonesome mode of life, when wealth and kindred had alike decayed or deserted. Such thoughts recurred naturally again to my mind as I and the old landlord descended from the hired hack, and entered the gates of Trinity Church, to pay the last honors to the body of poor Wigglesworth, who, at a heavy cost, had the one engrossing wish to be buried there with his mother. For his family, particularly on the maternal side, was of considerable rank, reduced as the old man had become.

May the aged clerk rest in peace there, in that vault in the midst of the clang and hubbub of the mighty city, which surrounds him on all sides! For his was a good nature; and from first to last, he had proved my firm friend. I often imagine him, even now that time has mellowed down his appearance—I often imagine him to be again shuffling around—his lips caved in upon a mouth bereft of teeth; his white, thin hair, his bent shoulders, his spectacles, and his dismally warm clothes. Again I say, may he rest in peace there in the venerable church-yard.

The better feeling of our times has created ample and tasteful cemeteries, at a proper distance from the turmoil of the town; the elegant and sombre Greenwood, unsurpassed probably in the world for its chaste and appropriately sober beauty; the varied and wooded slopes of the cemetery of the Evergreens; and the elevated and classic simplicity of Cypress Hills. And correct sanitary notions have properly made interments in the city limits illegal, prohibiting them by a fine which is heavy enough to form an effectual bar, except in cases, as occasionally happens even yet, of a strong desire to be buried in a spot hallowed by past associations and the presence of ancestors; with an ability to pay the fine.

Still, the few old grave-yards that lie in some of the busiest parts of our city, are not without their lesson; and a valuable one. On the occasion of the old man's scanty funeral, after the others had departed, and I was left alone, I spent the rest of that pleasant, golden forenoon, one of the finest days in our American autumn, wandering slowly through the Trinity grave-yard. I felt in the humor, serious without deep sadness, and I went from spot to spot, and sometimes copied the inscriptions. Long, rank grass covered my face. Over me was the verdure, touched with brown, of trees nourished from the decay of the bodies of men.

The tomb-stone nearest me held this inscription:

"JAMES M. BALDWIN,
"Aged 22 years,
"Wounded on Lake Champlain."

By the date of the time of his wound, and also that of his death, both of which were given on the stone, I knew that the latter took place about a year after the first. Here, then, lay one of the republic's faithful children—faithful to death. Was it—for I felt in a musing vein—hard for him to die? Hung round about his prospects a gay-colored future? Twenty-two: that was my own age—and, of Death, I shuddered instinctively at the thought!

For I felt that life, matter of fact as it was and is in reality—I felt that to me it opened enjoyment and pleasure on every side. I was happy in my friends—happy in having Ephraim and Violet and Tom and Martha and Inez—every one of them! I was happy that I lived in this glorious New York, where, if one goes without activity and enjoyment, it must be his own fault in the main.

Truly, life is sweet to the young man.—Such bounding and swelling capacities for joy reside within him, and such ambitious yearnings. Health and unfettered spirits are his staff and mantle. He learns unthinkingly to love—that glorious privilege of youth! Out of the tiny fractions of his experience, he builds beautiful imaginings, and confidently looks for the future to realize them. And then he is so sure of those future years.

Was not, probably, such the spirit of the young man whose grave I now sat on? The shroud and the coffin for *him*? Alas, so it was ordained. For nearly a year, fever burned his blood, and sharp pains racked him, and then came the dismissal of oblivion.

In the northern part of the old grave-yard I found the tombs of a father and mother, natives of New York, with a numerous family of their children. Haply, the whole of the chain, unbroken, was there. Various as I saw by the dates, were the periods of their dying, they had all been brought here at last, some of them, no doubt, from distant places, and were there mouldering, but together.

Human souls are as the dove, which went forth from the ark, and wandered far, and would repose herself at last on no spot save that whence she started. To what purpose has nature given men this instinct to die where they were born? Exists there some subtle sympathy between the thousand mental and physical essences which make up a human being, and the sources where from they are derived?

Another inscription I found in the grave yard read thus:

“EDWARD MARSHALL;

“*Died* 1704.”

The stone was low and uneven. The words appeared to

have been obliterated by time, and then traced out again by some kindly hand.

1704! at the time when these paragraphs are being printed, nearly a century and a half ago. Of the generations then upon the earth, probably not a person is living. What great events have happened too, since that time! A nation of freemen has arisen, out-stripping all ever before known in happiness, good government, and real grandeur. And even that star of Corsica which flitted like a glaring phantom across the world, now lies in no warmer a tomb, splendid as it is in the gay capital of France, than the one covered by that brown and age-decayed slab.

Near the wall that divides the yard from Rector-street, I stopped by the grave of a man, who, in his time, was the sower of seeds that have brought forth good and evil.

The burial stone tells the following story:

"TO THE MEMORY OF
"ALEXANDER HAMILTON.

"The Corporation of Trinity Church have erected this Monument in testimony of their respect for the patriot of incorruptible integrity, the soldier of approved valor, the statesman of consummate wisdom, whose talents and virtues will be admired by a grateful posterity, long after this marble shall have mouldered into dust."

The circumstances of the death of Hamilton, which took place July 12th, 1804, are well known. He was forty-seven years old. On the day of his funeral, the Common Council, the Militia, the Clergy, the Bar, and the Society of the Cincinnati, with a mass of citizens, convened in Park Place, and while dire wishes of vengeance rankled in many a bosom, moved in solemn procession down Broadway to Trinity Church, where Governeur Morris mounted a stage and erected in the portico, and delivered a funeral oration. The grief of Hamilton's family, who were present, seemed contagious; every eye was wet with tears. I may here add that I have once to twice in my time met the still living widow of the dead man—a lady whose aged form is constantly busied in works of kindness and benevolence.

Nearer to Broadway is a broad, square, simply elegant mausoleum, on the slab of which is graved:

"MY MOTHER:
"The trumpet shall sound,
"And the dead shall rise."

A sweet epitaph, and the manifestation of a most sweet motive!

In the farther corner of the yard was a ruined tomb, the bricks fallen down, and the whole partly covered by a rough pine shed. But read the history inscribed upon it:

"In memory of Capt. JAMES LAWRENCE, of the U. S. Navy, who fell on the first day of June 1813, in the 32d year of his age, in the action between the frigates *Chesapeake* and *Shannon*. * * * * He had distinguished himself on various occasions, but particularly while commanding the sloop of war *Hornet*, by capturing and sinking His Brit. Maj. sloop of war *Peacock*, after a desperate action of 14 minutes. His bravery in action was only equalled by his modesty in triumph, and his magnanimity to the vanquished. In private life, he was a gentleman of the most generous and endearing qualities, and so acknowledged was his public worth that the whole nation mourned his loss—and the enemy contended with his countrymen who should do him honor."

(*On the opposite side*)

"The hero whose remains are here deposited, with his dying breath expressed his devotion to his country. . . Neither the fury of the battle—the anguish of a mortal wound—nor the horrors of approaching death—could subdue his gallant spirit. His dying words were, *Don't give up the ship*!"

[In the present condition of the church and grounds, the remains of Lawrence have been removed from their distant corner, and now occupy a new and appropriate tomb, close by Broadway, at the immediate left of the lower gate. The foregoing inscription has been transferred literally; and the posts at the corners of the new tomb are formed of cannon planted there.]

Lawrence! the brave ideal of such as I—of all American young men!—what a day must that have been when he drew out of Boston harbor, and the hearts of his countrymen beat high with the confidence of victory. What a moment, when, struck down by the enemy's fire—enveloped in smoke and blood—the sounds and sights of carnage around him on every side—he was borne from the deck, overcome but not conquered—his last thought, his last gasp, given for his country! Taken by generous victors to Halifax, his corpse was treated with those testimonials of illustrious merit which became his exalted courage, and the character of a people never niggard in their admiration of true patriotism. But not long could his beloved republic spare the remains of a child so dear to her, and so fit to be a copy for her children. His body was brought to New York and here the people buried him. Even his nearest friends wept not. Their hearts were not sad, but joyful. The flag he died for, wrapped his coffin—and he was lowered in that native earth whose boast is that she has nurtured such brave defenders as himself.

Sleep gently, Bold Sailor! nor let it be thought presumptuous that many a youth of America, wandering near your ashes, feels that he could wish to emulate your devotion to your Native Land.

More and more enamored with these researches, I continued strolling for hours in the old place. Since the settlement of our island, this spot has never been used for any other than religious purposes. Before 1696 there was but one Episcopal church here; and that, until 1740, the time of the Negro Plot, when it was burned, stood in the Fort, now one of the favorite public grounds, the Battery. In 1696, Trinity was built; in 1737 it was enlarged, and in

1776 it was burnt down in the great fire which destroyed a thousand houses, just after the battle of Brooklyn, the city falling into the hands of the British.

In 1788, when the country had become somewhat settled from the Revolution, Trinity church was rebuilt, its dimensions being a hundred and one feet by seventy-four—a great size for those days. But the immense wealth of the church corporation, and the gigantic progress of the city, encouraged the officers—it is, when this statement is read, not many years ago—to pull down what was not yet an old edifice, and erect the costly and superb pile that certainly forms one of the finest pieces of architecture in the New World.

While pursuing my meditations, the noon had passed, and the after-half of the day crept onward; and it was time for me to close my ramble, and move homeward. I put my pencil and the slip of paper on which I had been copying, in my pocket, and took one slow and last look around, ere I went forth again into the city, and to resume my interest in affairs that lately so crowded upon me.

Out there in the fashionable thoroughfare, how bustling was life, and how jauntily it wandered close along the side of those warnings of its inevitable end. How gay that throng along the walk! Light laughs come from them, and jolly talk—those groups of well-dressed young men—those merry boys returning from school—clerks going home from their labors—and many a form, too, of female grace and elegance.

Could it be that coffins, six feet below where I stood, enclosed the ashes of like young men, whose vestments, during life, had engrossed the same anxious care—and schoolboys and beautiful women; for they too were buried here, as well as the aged and infirm.

But onward rolled the broad, bright current, and troubled themselves not yet with gloomy thoughts; and that showed more philosophy in them perhaps than such sentimental meditations as any the reader has been perusing.

CHAPTER XX.

I spend an evening in the perusal of the manuscript.

NOT A WORD from Covert. Was not the silence ominous? But any way, Martha was out of his power; and we had that important possession which is nine points of the law.

Ephraim heard from Hoboken in the course of the day. All went smoothly there. Nathaniel came in on his way home, to say that the office, with the exception of himself and his dog, was quite deserted, he also having received, from his master, no word or command that day.

I did not altogether like this stillness, for I feared Covert's craft, and, that there might be something behind, of which I was not yet aware. My reflections convinced me, however, that there was no better course for our side, than to keep quiet, and let the enemy make his move for himself.

The hour was yet early when I retired to my room that night, and placed my lamp on the table. I had been pretty seriously impressed with the occurrences of the past few days, and with the reflections in the graveyard of Old Trinity. I took from the drawer, where I had deposited it, the manuscript written by the unfortunate father of the Quakeress; for I felt that I was in a fitting temper to read it.

When I had removed the envelope, and opened it, I found the manuscript written in a hasty and often scrawling manner, evidently under the influence of excitement. It was upon the strong stiff paper used many years since, and still remained in perfect preservation.

That it interested me completely, and that I felt a deep sympathy for the unfortunate gentleman who had committed it to paper, is certain. Time and his punishment obliterated any thing that might otherwise have been resentment in my feelings toward him; and his story came to me more like something I might read in a book. The tone of the narrative is morbid, but under the circumstances that must of course be expected.

NARRATIVE OF MARTHA'S FATHER.

Whoever you are, into whose hands this dismal story may fall—oh, let me hope that my daughter may read it, and drop a tear for her parent—whoever you are, whether daughter, friend, or stranger, I begin my narrative, written in prison, to while away the heavy hours and leave the chance of one little legacy of sympathy for myself, by a command.

Look around you on the beautiful earth, the free air, sky, fields and streets—the people swarming in all directions.—All this is common you say; it is not worth a thought I once supposed thus, like you. But I suppose so no longer. Now all these things seem to me the most beautiful objects in the world. To be free, to walk where you will—to look on freedom—to be free from care, too—by which I mean, not to have your soul pressed down by the weight of horrible odium or disgrace; not to have a dreadful punishment hanging over you—O, that is happiness.

Happiness! Alas, what absurdities pass among men, under the name.

Happiness: I am in prison, with death perhaps waiting for me; and I write some of my thoughts on happiness.

Is there, indeed, no specific for the enjoyment of life? Come we here on earth but to toil and sorrow—to eat, drink, and beget children—to sicken and die? In that world, the heart of man, glisten no sun-rays and bloom no blossoms, as in the outer world? And love, and ambition, and intellect, and wealth—fountains whence, in youth, we expect the future years to draw so much of this happiness—as their fruition comes, does not disappointment also come?

I would that the Devil in the garden of Eden had been made to tell the young man what it was that led to felicity. That in these modern days, the pursuits in which men engage with so much ardor—the men all around us—do not reach it, is evidence.—Wealth cannot purchase it. The newspapers every month contain accounts of individuals, assuredly prosperous in all their pecuniary affairs, and some of them young and healthy, who in the very midst of what the poor think perfect bliss, have committed self-murder. The successful seeker after rank and place is not happy,—not from that success, at least. The most learned scholars are often the most melancholy men in the world. Beauty grieves and pines as much as the brain which wears a homely face. Elegant dress frequently covers a sick soul—and the furniture of a handsome carriage may be but the trappings of misery.

Then among the busier and more laboring kinds of people, the same general absence of happiness prevails. It seems reasonable that he whose existence is one uninterrupted struggle to keep off starvation by slavery and hard work at that—should see but few bright days. But the man whose labors are effectual, fares little better. The mechanic, the ploughman, the literary drudge, are alike debarred from any delicious experience of that sweet morsel we so much prize, but never obtain. I am speaking now, not of the goodly gratifications of sense or everyday tastes, which are common enough—but of the attainment, at any time, to that condition when a man can say to himself, I feel perfect bliss, I have no desire ungratified.

Am I not philosophic here in my grated walls? Do you not see how keen my sight has become? And truly it is a consolation, in this sort, to think what a miserable world it is.

But I would not be miserable if I had one great weight off my soul, and were at liberty again. Now, when I am nigh leaving life my eyes are just opened to its beauty; O, what a cheap and common beauty! To be free, and not to be a criminal!

For I have now also removed the greatest bar that once stood between me and happiness; that was a fiery temper. I have lost that now; I feel that if I should live a hundred years, they would be a hundred years without anger or revenge.

How wild, how disconnected are my tho'ts. How I talk of a hundred years! Shall I see, yet half a hundred days?

A fiery temper grew up in me from my birth. My boyhood was fierce and uncontrolled; my home was not worthy the name; I had no home. Although parents cared enough for me to spend money liberally, and give me an almost unlimited indulgence that way, yet they did not furnish me what is most wanted from parents—good example, good counsel and a true home-roof. I was boarded, almost from the beginning, away in the country.

For I had such a stormy temper; and my mother was nervous, and the servants would not stand it. And the father, Ah, he meddled himself with no such things, and did not even want to be spoke to about them. Was he not at all the expense? Could he not fairly count that enough? Besides, I was to inherit his property; that must satisfy me. It were too much to expect that he should give up his time for my education, and the shaping of my character. Even the death of my mother, which occurred when I was a half grown boy, made no difference in his treatment.

Such are what the world calls good parents; for they do not beat their children, nor starve them. They leave them estates too, and what does a child want more than money?

When I grew up to be a young man, I was rude, boisterous, and ungovernable. Already I had fallen into many scrapes, from my violent temper; but they were none of them hard enough to teach me the great lesson I needed. My temper was made, indeed, rather more unbearable from them; for I emerged victorious after all.

One gleam of sunshine came across my life, and, for a time, subdued me into gentler condition. Love tamed me from my roughness. She was herself a being of peace and calmness—she whom I loved; and her influence brought into my temperament something of the same soothing qualities. She was of Quaker family; and perhaps it was that the very tameness to which she had been accustomed gave my free and independent manner the charm of freshness, to her taste.

For my affection was returned, truly and faithfully. She did not chance to see the worst phases of my character. Her very presence was soothing and pacifying. For never did I dissemble. I acted always as I felt; and had the occasion provoked, not even the knowledge of what an ungracious look it would possess in her eyes, could have kept down my rebellious temper.

My father had an attack of illness at this time which, in the course of a few weeks, was pronounced hopeless. I did not mourn; for what reason had I? He called me to him before he died, and, at the eleventh hour, gave me some good advice. Some good advice—some words! Doubtless they were very valuable—those words; but they were nothing but words. After the tree has grown up, with the bend in its trunk, and the shape of its branches formed, would it do to stand before it and preach a sermon of good advice? Would it change that bend, or the gnarled branches?

But a few months passed away after my father's death, when I found myself married and comfortably settled. Ah, those were my happiest days. These tears that roll down my cheeks while I write, attest it. They are not bitter tears. The time of which they are the remembrance, is the only gleam of pure light in the course of my past career of cloudy chequered fortune. And, sweet as it was—that long continued honey moon—the saving freshness it brings to me now, is perhaps the most beautiful part of it! It illumines this prison cell. It bestows a charmed atmosphere even in these sad and sombre walls.

A child, too, blessed our marriage, a fair daughter. May she be blessed, in her life, with something of that blessing which she brought to us. May she live, and, when she looks back on these dismal days, and the tears drop for her ill-fated father, ah, then perhaps the story of my life will have its office in her mind.

I commenced this document with some gloomy thoughts on happiness. But gloomy as they are, and fitted for my present situation, I am almost tempted to blot them out.

The memory of the twenty months that followed my marriage is a full denial of him who would say there is no happiness on earth. Surely my good genius was in the ascendent all that time. Oh how soon it was to be followed by a thunderstroke!

There was a man of my own age, but poor and hardy, whom I had known while we were boys together, when I was boarding in the country. He had in many things been my friend; but, even when youngsters, we frequently quarrelled, for he would never submit to my domineering temper. He belonged to what are termed the common classes, and, as I had wealth, perhaps it was that which separated us afterward. For I met him often in the city to which he had himself come, and was earning his living, in a poor way. Illiterate, hard-working, and married to an ordinary and rather shiftless woman, he was not much worse off, when his wife died and left him a widower with a little infant son.

My evil genius it was that put this man in my way. His hard life had formed him to a temper as morose as mine was fiery. He occupied part of a mean dwelling close in the neighborhood of my own costly residence; and various causes conspired to bring us into contact. I had not thought of it before; but it seemed to me now, notwithstanding the little services of friendship which he had performed for me, that there had always been some seeds of antipathy between us. He made sarcastic remarks about my appearance and manners. He thought I was, from vulgar pride, unwilling to acknowledge the former intimacy with him. He was mistaken in the cause, although right in his conclusion.

I gave out a contract to make some additions and repairs on my premises; and this man was engaged by the contractor, in a laboring capacity, among his workmen. I was too proud to utter a word about it; but his appearance was greatly annoying to me. He took a bitter advantage, too, of the position he had, relative to mine; and often was I conscious of his sneers and jibes, as I passed along, followed by the suppressed laughter of the workmen.

This was all a trifle, it may seem; and so indeed it was. But that man made, to me, the Jew sitting in the King's gate; a living mockery to my pride.

One time when his remarks were coldly insolent to my face, I swore to him that if he repeated his unprovoked outrages, I would dash him to the earth.

He laughed tauntingly, but at that time replied not a word. I was conscious, at the while, that I cut a poor figure before the men who surrounded us; and that added to my vexation.

A few days later—O dismal hour!—I went through the newly building part, with the boss, giving directions and receiving explanations of the proposed work. We had got through talking and I was about to leave the place, when I heard one of this man's sarcasms upon me—upon my pride, and even about some peculiarities of my person. The boss had left, unfortunately; although the workmen were all around. I suppressed my anger, which was suddenly rising; and even turned to leave the place. I had to pass my enemy on the way.

He enjoyed his triumph, and just as I was passing him, he coolly and deliberately spoke to me words of still deeper and more provoking influence than ever he had uttered before; and directly addressed them to me with the evident design of cutting me to the quick.

My blood was already afire in my veins; and this maddened me. I hardly remember now with sufficient distinctness what passed. I think I had gone a couple of steps beyond where the man stood; but the fury was too much, then. I turned, made one spring upon him, and, in the rage of my anger wrenched from his hand the mallet he had been working with, and dealt him a blow directly on top of the head!

My arm was unnaturally nerved by an insane ferocity. It was the stroke of death. He fell like a log, and I stood there a murderer!

The ensuing few hours are like a hateful and confused dream to me. I was neither asleep nor awake. I felt a sort of numbness and remember closing and shutting my eyes incessantly. I did not stir from the spot, during the horror, and the outcries, and hurry and dread of the immediate half-hour that followed the murder. I stood and looked on the poor fellow's body, and I thought, strangely enough, of us two, when we were boys together; when we had often gone out fishing, and swimming, and gunning together. I thought of the services he had done me, and remembered what a brave boy he was, and how, in any trouble, he never deserted me then, but stood as staunch as steel. Even the little incidents of our country life came up before me; our friendship—the fences where we crossed—the orchards—the shores—the old leaky scow—the hickory poles that were used for fishing-rods.

Could it be that I, now, was the murderer of that boy? Even the thought of my own condition and of my wife and little daughter, was crowded aside by such remembrances as these; they came slowly and turgidly floating through the current of my mind.

A wild despairing shriek—it rings in my ears now!—roused me from my reverie. Oh, that terrible cry; it was the agony of a broken hearted wife—of a soul crushed to powder, by one stroke!

She breathed my name—whispered it faintly and lovingly. Her ghastly face, with a frightful dampness upon it, turned toward me, and yearningly in the weakness of her sinews, endeavored to reach up to my own sweating features. I lifted her, pressed one long tight kiss upon her lips, and then resigned her inanimate form to those, who bore her to the bed where she lay unconscious of life or sorrow for twice twenty hours. Then this pure souled creature died as a flower might wilt of a chilly evening, silently, and without complaint.

I made no effort to escape, and I think I did not utter a word to the officers who guarded me to prison. An awful blank seemed to spread through the mental part of me; cold—cold as ice, without any action, or object, or warmth. It was not painful—at least, not beyond a dull, deadened sense of something like fulness which oppressed my head.

One hour! what a change it had made for me.

I was not treated with any roughness, either by the crowd who gathered quickly to the spot, or by the policemen. Some of the work people gave a true statement of the insolence of the poor fellow I had slain, and how it was done in the sudden fury of the moment. They made the case as favorable to me as they could, and the appearance, and overwhelmed sorrow of my poor wife, completed the work of compassionate feeling toward me. Tears fell down many a weather-beaten cheek, and haply many a silent prayer was offered up for the wretched young man whose days were darkened with even a drearier fate than had befallen the poor victim there.

And so, I was in prison, a murderer.

For my wife's death I felt no deep regret; to die was less grief than to live, I knew, in her case. Ah! was it not so in my own?

The law, which is often cruel in minor accusations, is seldom so in great ones. I have been treated fairly and honorably here in my prison. Whatever indulgence could properly be given has not been denied me.—There is a noble pity that frequently actuates jailers and officers of the law, toward the wretched ones who come under their charge, on their path to heavy punishment—a pity, beautiful and honorable to their characters, and showing well in them. This compassion I experienced throughout, and it made me think better of my kind.

After the first deadening numbing night passed, the next morning, when the day dawned upon me here where I am now writing, I was a changed man. I felt composed enough, and indeed was without any of that anxious dread which might be supposed natural to one in my situation. At the same time, I was fully conscious of that situation. It was all present to me, and I comprehended every point of it. The crime, its legal punishment, the poor victim, my family, the lamentable violence of my former temper, the scene and incidents of the murder, the best points in my behalf—all were clearly arrayed before my thought. My *former* temper, I say; for I looked back, now, upon that as pertaining to a separate existence. I knew that, under any conceivable circumstances, it was mine no longer. The serpent had cast his slough.

A legal agent whom I had formerly employed, I picked out from several whose names I turned over in my mind, and sent for him. He was an honorable man, I felt sure, from his conduct when I employed him. Much to my sorrow, he was absent on a voyage of considerable distance. An answer to this effect has been brought me by a lawyer, who, some years ago, had studied, he tells me, in the office of the absent attorney. Would it not be a good thought to engage this man, for some of my small commissions at least? I questioned myself. His countenance is impassive; but he is a Quaker, and that fact recommends him to me.

* * I have commissioned the man, whose name is Covert, to see to the decent burial of my poor victim, and have

given him written authority, and command of funds, for that, and a few other purposes.

Many of my hours are occupied with the arrangement of my worldly affairs; for there has come to me a notion, amounting to a certainty, that I am dying! Friends to whom I have mentioned this fear, endeavor to chase it away by saying that it is the result of my brooding thoughts; and that such vagaries often come into the minds of people under a great dread. I do not answer them, but I feel none the less the certainty of my death. Nor is it painful to me.

[Here a blank, the next part of the manuscript being on another page.]

My will has been duly drawn up with minuteness. I have left the bulk of my fortune to my daughter, and a goodly portion of it, properly secured, to the child of my victim.

Covert comes to me every day. He strongly advises me to make preparations for my trial, to engage the best legal talent, and so forth. He almost sneers at me, when I answer that nothing of the sort is needed.

He is a doubtful creature—this, neither old nor young lawyer; I hardly know what to make of him. Upon the whole, however, I have concluded to trust him; he is now thoroughly advised of my intentions and affairs. I am particularly induced, to make him my friend; for his wife, much older than himself, who is gentle and good, if there be any such qualities on earth, has shown the tenderest affection for my little child, whom she has consented to take charge of. She has no children, and treats my poor helpless one with all a mother's affection.

* * * The day approaches. I have made all my preparations, and I feel now calmer than at any time since I have dwelt in this prison. Should I think of any thing more I will add it; if not, let whoever reads this dark story know that I experience, while I write, more composure and rest than any day I recall during the years of my ordinary life, with the exception of my marriage time. I do not doubt that I am dying.

My little daughter; may Heaven protect her unprotected childhood. May God pity me, and may I continue to feel this soothing calm to the last.

[Here was a long blank; and the paragraph that follows was written evidently by another hand, at another time.]

The prayer uttered in the last lines by my dear and unfortunate friend was not in vain. He retained his equanimity, and his forebodings were strangely verified. The day set down for his trial found him dead; that very day he was committed to the grave. He charged me with the narrative he had written, and intended for his daughter, should she live, as he had every confidence she would, and grow to womanhood.

[The remaining part of the paper, which filled several pages, in the same hand as the last paragraph, consisted of some references, legal data, and religious advice; all of which would not be of interest.]

CHAPTER XXI.

Setting forth the conduct of Mr. Covert when he found himself in a tight place.

THE FOILED LAWYER—the fox caught in a trap while he thought he had so nicely fixed traps for others! It was not an agreeable picture to look upon, but I will portray it, as, I afterward learnt to my satisfaction, the reality transpired.

Covert did not know of Martha's departure, till early in the morning; but then his suspicious soul immediately felt that something was wrong—and something serious too. It was never the custom for Martha to leave the house in that way; and where had she to go without informing him?

Sick before, and now doubly sick with alarm, he instinctively hobbled to what he supposed the safe repository of his valuable plunder—supposed, and yet had an indefinite sort of fear.

Miserable, pale, wretch! there was something in the electric shock of despair and baffled selfishness, condensed in that first minute of confusion, to revenge upon you the scores of villainies you had perpetrated, commencing with the swindle of the poor carpenter.

That long life of lies and cheats for gain, came like a flash before him!

And now, after all, to be foiled!

With trembling hands, his forehead running a chill sweat, the lawyer commenced turning out everything. Perhaps he had misplaced the precious documents, and they were there yet. He ransacked high and low. He went over the search again; and, dropping his cane, for he felt an unnatural strength suddenly come into his weakened veins, he began a systematic search through the room, in its every part.

He was desperate, indeed. What chance was there?

No matter, he finished that room, and then went over the next in the same manner. And then the next.

At last he ascended to Martha's apartment. Her furniture, and many of her things were there, as formerly; but it was evident that she had made a careful selection of what she most needed; and those articles were taken away.

He called up the servant from the kitchen. She was a stupid, half-witted girl, the only help he kept in the place. She could give him no information, for she had been soundly sleeping when Martha departed.

Obtaining a messenger, he sent down at once to the office, for me to come up to his house. Far from being at the office, I had, when I put my hat on my head the evening before, taken an oath never voluntarily to enter its doors again. My days of studying law, I felt, might as well come to an end; and, since these revelations, Ephraim Foster did not seem to entertain the old obstinacy that way.

"After all, Jack," he had said that morning, "I don't know but I was too fast in pushing you to this sort of life. The Lord forgive me if you should lose your honesty by it!"

I seriously assured him that I could not answer for myself; and that I already felt a sort of nibbling disposition in the points of my fingers.

Covert's messenger was instructed, in default of me, to bring up Wigglesworth, if he could be brought, or, as a last resort, the boy Nathaniel.

Wigglesworth was on his death-bed; and thus it fell that my spirited young friend of the night before, whistling to his dog, coolly clapt his hat on his head and bade the messenger—whom he styled "my son," although that personage was old enough to be his grandfather—go on before, and convey to Mr. Covert an assurance of his love, and that he would be with the good man forthwith.

Nathaniel, who locked the door, and carried the key in his hand, had much to attract his attention on his journey. In the first place, he came round to me, according to a previous arrangement, and told me that he had been sent for, and was going.

"And it's my opinion," said Nat, "that I shall take the opportunity to let the old boy into a piece of my mind."

I cautioned him against mentioning the whereabouts of Martha, just at present. With respect to any further information he might say as much as he liked.

He took his walk very leisurely, except where there was a provoking chance to have a race with Jack. There were the theatre bills to read; these he perused with close attention, from top to bottom. There were the various turn-outs in the street—particularly every trim and stylish nag, attached to a buggy or sulkey, the least bit of a flash description. Of all the world such a possession was the envy and engrossing ambition of the boy's heart. He strained his eyes, then, as far as the horse could be seen.

Since he had grown a little older, Nathaniel was not so pugnacious as formerly; and though he took interest enough in any personal conflict that happened to fall under his attention, he no more felt the old itching to take part in it himself, unless where specially invited or called upon.

When Nat arrived at Mr. Covert's house, he refused the girl's request to leave Jack out in the front area; unless his friend were admitted, he, Nathaniel, would not be persuaded to pass the door.

He was shown into the room, and there found himself face to face with Covert; and standing by the window were Ferris and the dandy Smytthe. The feverish impatience of the lawyer could not be controlled; and fast upon the heels of the first messenger was dispatched a second with order for those two worthies.

"Where's Engle?" said Covert to the boy at once.

"As near as I can tell," answered Nat, "Mr. Engle is at his residence, or dwelling."

"Wigglesworth, I hear, is very bad—no hopes of living."

Nat inclined his head.

"What's been going on at the office?" continued Covert, looking sharply at the boy.

That young gentleman merely repeated the question.

"Yes; who has been there? Why is Engle not there? Do you know anything of Martha? Have you heard any thing?"

The excited lawyer hurried question upon question, and sat down breathless.

"Well now," said Nat, composedly, "I guess you are flustered. Martha has left you, hasn't she?"

Covert sprung from his seat again, and made as if he would seize Nat bodily. The dog bristled up, and uttered a low growl.

"It'll do no good to get flustered," continued Nat, "I know Martha's gone, as well as you do. And I know she'll never come back again. And I know Mr. Engle will never come back again. And what do you say, if I tell you that I am going and shall never come back again?"

"It would be a good riddance of an idle and impertinent young scamp," said Covert sternly; although he now suppressed any more violent evidences of passion, and motioned the boy to the door; for he saw that he was going to get nothing from him.

Nat, after daintily placing the key on the table retired

with a mock bow, wishing the lawyer better judgment of people's characters, and hoping he would begin to pass a pleasant night, as soon as it came dark.

What passed in the conference between the three worthies who were left, I never learned. That they were, to a great extent, implicated together in plans of villainy, there is no doubt; and thus were bound to afford each other mutual help in time of need.

The rest of that day, and during the night—while we were expecting every moment to hear something from Covert, and wondering why we did not—there was bustle and activity about the lawyer's house. Pepperich Ferris and Smytthe were in and out,—and in and out again; several times making long journeys up and down from the house to the office, and from the office to the house.

No help was called in from outside; a few little purchases were left at the door, where they were taken in by Smytthe, and there was a noise of nailing up boxes, and tumbling things from room to room.

At the closing of the afternoon of the day subsequent to Nathaniel's visit, the same young gentleman, being then at leisure, happened to circulate through the very street again, and in front of Covert's house, which he passed by on the opposite side. A carriage was waiting at the door, and the boy naturally stopped to see what it meant.

Presently, down the steps came Mr. Covert, assisted by Ferris. He entered the carriage alone; and Nat saw that it was crowded with trunks and carpet bags. Before the youngster well recovered from his astonishment, the driver was up on his box, and the hack dashed away at a rapid rate. Ferris deliberately ascended the steps, locked the door, tried it again to see if all was right, went down and tried the basement door also, stood a moment on the walk in front, and scanned the tightly closed blinds, and then walked musingly away.

Nat was at his wit's end to find a clue to Covert's destination; for the sharp-witted youth knew that I would in all probability be anxious to know. He accosted the woman of a little shop, in front of the spot whence he had observed these movements. But all that she knew, notwithstanding her curiosity had also been on the alert, was, that a big cart full of trunks and well-packed articles taken away two hours before, was destined for the Albany boat.

Nat sprang off at a venture for the pier region, down town, in hopes of getting further information. And never had Jack been more perseveringly rivalled in the race than this pleasant hour in the decline of the afternoon.

The boy was too late to reach the boat. He saw the carriage, however, and promptly stopping the driver, who had deposited his passenger on board the steamer some fifteen minutes before, he learned that the trunks of that bilious and wrinkle-faced man, who seemed laboring under a restless excitement, and spoke so faintly, and trembled so much, were marked not only for Albany, but for a distant town in Canada! And Covert, he heard asking one of the clerks of the boat, how long it would necessarily take him to reach that place—the best means of getting there—and the shortest possible time.

Yes; the enemy fairly fled, and left us in possession of the field. And, strange as it may appear, we never heard anything definite from or about Covert, after that departure. We never even knew whether he reached his destination alive.

As to Pepperich Ferris and Smytthe, they doubtless had good reasons for keeping close tongues in their mouths. They would not favor the numerous anxious inquirers after their old friend with a single item of explanation; but swore that they didn't know what became of the runaway, any more than other people.

CHAPTER XXII.

In which we all get to the end of the journey.

THE HISTORY OF my adventures draws to its conclusion. I have not much more to tell, and that I will dispatch quickly.

It was natural enough that the love which had its rise in my mind toward the young Quakeress, should take a course usual in such matters. But I forego the infliction of a courtship, on whoever has travelled with me thus far.—My attachment was returned; and, in a few months after the last of the events already recorded, Violet, much to her satisfaction, gave my wedding supper to a few choice friends.

The investigations of Wigglesworth had been so thorough, and he had so completely noted down, with date and volume and page, and every other particular, the links in the chain of evidence to substantiate the truth of Martha's rights, and of the history, as far as was needed in law, that has been narrated in the foregoing chapters—of the father and his death, together with his will and disposition of his property—all these were so minutely detailed, and substantiated by references to authentic records of the courts, and other unquestionable data, that we found no difficulty in settling the whole matter to our satisfaction.

Martha had no near relative; and the few distant ones of whom she had heard, after her being taken charge of by Mrs. Covert, who seems to have been the very antipodes of her husband,—even those far-away connections had lost sight of her, and she was left to depend much upon the good lady who, through her most helpless years, acted as her best friend and protector.

The very means which the lawyer had hit upon to carry out his own wicked designs, proved ultimately to be in our favor. I allude to the turning of so much of Martha's property into bonds and paper, as more convenient for transportation or concealment. The valuable bills and documents we had, in the manner before stated, secured possession of.

That Covert made no attempt against his former ward, after her flight, is not perhaps surprising. He knew that she now had devoted friends; and that a legal investigation would result in an unavoidable exposure not at all to his credit. Besides, this would in all likelihood draw in its train other investigations and exposures, involving his schemes in conjunction with Ferris. To dismiss him here, I will add, that from his distant Canada residence we never had any positive intelligence of him; and were satisfied best that it was so.

Inez, for the few days that Martha staid with her, showed

all her natural goodness and generosity. Was it stopped a little, when she saw, with female quickness, the sentiment that had grown up between Martha and myself? If so, it made no difference in her treatment of the Quakeress; and she was one of the liveliest of the merry company at my wedding supper.—Whether Mr. Thomas Peterson consoled the excellent and really fine-hearted girl, I cannot aver of my own knowledge; but it was evident that they rapidly became great friends with one another.

With the advance of the season, too, Inez was busy in her preparations for a professional tour; she having engagements that way. This tour engrossed her time and attention, and proved, I understand, a very profitable one.

Tom Peterson's friendship—the noble and always welcome young man!—has not been lost to me by marriage. He is much engaged in his trade as a machinist, which he is enthusiastically fond of; and he has become invaluable to the proprietors of the large establishment where he was foreman. The establishment is now merged in the property of a company, with far greater capital, and the business much enlarged and perfected; Tom being advanced to a station of still greater confidence and trust, with a handsome salary to back it.

Although this responsible post fills up his time pretty well, Tom finds leisure of a Sunday to come out in the stage to the cottage where we—for I cut any further connection with the law—have settled ourselves, at a little distance from the city—and where we spend the summer.

May your life be sunshiny, Tom Peterson, and the end of it a long while away!

Ephraim Foster and Violet are well satisfied with all these developments; as, indeed, they are not easily induced to worry themselves, with the course of affairs, so long as they have their health and a good living, and see their friends in the enjoyment of the same blessings. That beautiful philosophy! what a pity it is, that we do not see more of it, in this world of more imaginary than real troubles—great as the latter are.

Ephraim, although years have passed with him since the period when he is first introduced in this narrative, is about the same old two-and-sixpence. He sticks to his provision and grocery store—which, as I remarked in a previous chapter, has superseded the original milk and sausage line—and laughs at me when I propose to him to accept any pecuniary help, and retire from public life. No; that he will not do, at present, nor Violet either. They are very well satisfied; the employment just suits them, and the income is neither more or less than they want.

And although "No Trust" yet hangs up printed in white letters on a little dingy green board over the counter, Ephraim and Violet *do* trust, not only as much as in the early days, but a little more. Whenever the family is poor, or the father or mother sick; or when the appeal comes, as it often does, from some helpless widow, or even the wife of an intemperate husband—then neither does Ephraim put on a frown, nor Violet look the other way. The basket is silently heaped up, and there is no sulkiness, to take away the blessing of the deed. Thus do these two cast their bread upon the waters, in faith and true charity. And although they make no sanctimonious professions, will they not find it again returned to them after many days?

Violet, I think, grows really beautiful as she approaches the latter part of middle age. She is still as stout, strong, and healthy as ever, and—most important fact of all, which I ought to have jotted down before! during the years that I have been recording the events of the past narrative, has presented her lord and master with two hearty boys, one of whom is six and the other three years old; the biggest being named Jack Engle Foster. The advent and growth of these plump and jolly little fellows, however, and the interest taken in them by father and mother, never subtracted a particle from my own portion. And as to Master Jack, who always showed a tenacious attachment to me, he spends nearly the whole summer at our cottage. I look forward, at an early day, to the privilege of introducing him to some additional society. The young gentleman indeed, teases me now and then on this subject, and asks me whether I will not hurry and make "that little playfellow" for him. I have no way of answering, except to assure the child that I will do my best; and that I confidently promise the gift to him in due time. The persevering youngster then asks me whether it is already begun, and will only be satisfied with my direct assertion to that effect.

Nathaniel, too, and his canine friend, are occasionally among my visitors. Nat grows in grace daily, and has found a much better situation than the one he held in Covert's office. He will make a fast man, this Nat, when he grows big enough.

Calvin Peterson adheres faithfully to his professions, and continues to exercise his lungs at the revival meetings. I have before remarked that Calvin is a sincere worshipper, in his own way: and that's more than can be said of many of the children of the church.

Fitzmore Smytthe and Ferris, some time afterward, commenced business under the firm of Ferris & Co., Brokers. The last I heard of them, was, through a paragraph in the paper, in which they were hauled up before a Police Court, at the suit of a returned Californian, for some semi-swindling. They paid their fine, quietly took the rebuke of the Judge, and—kept on as before.

Barney and Nancy Fox regularly create an addition to the census, with each recurring year. Barney, since he got started, has grown into a man of means and importance. He is a thorough hand at electioneering, and possesses some advantages not commonly enjoyed in that profound science. There is even talk of putting Barney in nomination for quite an important municipal office.

Madame Seligny, almost on the heels of Covert's sudden departure, went abroad; she said, for the purpose of taking possession of an inheritance. What truth there was in that part of the stay I know not. But Rebecca accompanied her, and that forever broke up the pleasant intimacy between Tom Peterson and the pretty Jewess.

With everything promising fair for a life of health and comfort—though no one can tell what the future may bring forth; with blessings on my lot, and on those who have stood my friends when I most needed them; with good humor toward all the world, a heart full of satisfaction, and pockets that do not flutter from lightness—JACK ENGLE, here closeth the narrative of his LIFE and ADVENTURES.

THE IOWA WHITMAN SERIES

Conserving Walt Whitman's Fame: Selections from Horace Traubel's "Conservator," 1890–1919, edited by Gary Schmidgall

Democratic Vistas: The Original Edition in Facsimile, by Walt Whitman, edited by Ed Folsom

Intimate with Walt: Selections from Whitman's Conversations with Horace Traubel, 1888–1892, edited by Gary Schmidgall

Leaves of Grass, 1860: The 150th Anniversary Edition, by Walt Whitman, edited by Jason Stacy

A Place for Humility: Whitman, Dickinson, and the Natural World, by Christine Gerhardt

The Pragmatic Whitman: Reimagining American Democracy, by Stephen John Mack

Song of Myself*: With a Complete Commentary*, by Walt Whitman and introduction and commentary by Ed Folsom and Christopher Merrill

Supplement *to "Walt Whitman: A Descriptive Bibliography,"* by Joel Myerson

Transatlantic Connections: Whitman U.S., Whitman U.K., by M. Wynn Thomas

Visiting Walt: Poems Inspired by the Life and Work of Walt Whitman, edited by Sheila Coghill and Thom Tammaro

Walt Whitman and the Class Struggle, by Andrew Lawson

Walt Whitman and the Earth: A Study in Ecopoetics, by M. Jimmie Killingsworth

Walt Whitman: The Correspondence, Volume VII, edited by Ted Genoways

Walt Whitman, Where the Future Becomes Present, edited by David Haven Blake and Michael Robertson

Walt Whitman's Reconstruction: Poetry and Publishing between Memory and History, by Martin T. Buinicki

Walt Whitman's Selected Journalism, edited by Douglas A. Noverr and Jason Stacy

Walt Whitman's Songs of Male Intimacy and Love: "Live Oak, with Moss" and "Calamus," edited by Betsy Erkkila

Whitman among the Bohemians, edited by Joanna Levin and Edward Whitley

Whitman East and West: New Contexts for Reading Walt Whitman, edited by Ed Folsom

Whitman Noir: Black America and the Good Gray Poet, edited by Ivy G. Wilson

Whitman's Drift: Imagining Literary Distribution, by Matt Cohen